The Wind Traveler

D0113177

LATIN AMERICAN
LITERATURE IN
TRANSLATION SERIES

OTHER BOOKS IN THE SERIES

The Enlightened Army by David Toscana
Human Matter: A Fiction by Rodrigo Rey Rosa
The Last Days of El Comandante by Alberto Barrera Tyszka
Animals at the End of the World by Gloria Susana Esquivel

The Wind Traveler
A Novel

Alonso Cueto

Translated by Frank Wynne and Jessie Mendez Sayer

UNIVERSITY OF TEXAS PRESS

Austin

Original Spanish edition published by Editorial Planeta Perú in 2016 under the title
La viajera del viento, copyright © 2016 by Alonso Cueto
English translation © 2020 by the University of Texas Press
All rights reserved
Printed in the United States of America

Requests for permission to reproduce material from this work should be sent to:
    Permissions
    University of Texas Press
    P.O. Box 7819
    Austin, TX 78713-7819
    utpress.utexas.edu/rp-form

♾ The paper used in this book meets the minimum requirements of ANSI/NISO Z39.48-1992 (R1997) (Permanence of Paper).

Library of Congress Cataloging-in-Publication Data

Names: Cueto, Alonso, 1954– author. | Wynne, Frank, translator. | Sayer, Jessie Mendez, translator.
Title: The wind traveler : a novel / Alonso Cueto ; translated by Frank Wynne and Jessie Mendez Sayer.
Other titles: Viajera del viento. English
Description: First edition. | Austin : University of Texas Press, 2020. | Series: Latin American literature in translation | Identifiers: LCCN 2020004312
    ISBN 978-1-4773-1774-7 (paperback ; alk. paper)
    ISBN 978-1-4773-1775-4 (library ebook)
    ISBN 978-1-4773-1776-1 (non-library ebook)
Classification: LCC PQ8498.13.U34 V5313 2020 | DDC 863/.64—dc23
LC record available at https://lccn.loc.gov/2020004312

doi:10.7560/317747

For Francisco Lombardi, storyteller

Intillay killallay kanchay
Kamullaway, tullaypim
Purichkani mamallayta, taytallayta
(Sun and moon, shine your light on me
I am walking through darkness
searching for my mother and my father.)

VERSE FROM CAYARA CARNIVAL,
QUOTED BY KIMBERLY THEIDON IN
Intimate Enemies: Violence and Reconciliation in Peru

An illuminated memory, a gallery haunted by
the shadow of what I wait for.

ALEJANDRA PIZARNIK, *Diana's Tree*

I

The day Ángel decided to resign his army commission, he saw a dense, gentle drizzle that he took as a sign of approval from the city. He was going to lay down his arms and Lima, with its soft gray mantle, was rejoicing.

He had completed his military service beneath a harsh, dry sun, in a barracks on the outskirts of Ayacucho. Unsurprisingly, he preferred not to remember anything that had happened there. He had just returned, and no sooner did he arrive at the barracks in Chorrillos than he realized he could not carry on for even one more day.

At the army administration offices, Ángel discovered that he was entitled to a small pension for his years of service. He decided it was better to refuse it. He would have felt guilty taking the money, although he could not have said why. This decision meant he had to present new documents and write a special letter.

He went through the retirement paperwork at the office windows of a green building, with a man wearing a flannel shirt and suspenders. The routine was always the same. The man would acknowledge his greeting without looking up. Then he would examine the documents with his chipped nails. Eventually, he would scrawl notes in the margins in black ink. Sometimes, the man would run his finger under each line and would take some time to get to the end. But he invariably authorized the papers with all the stamps and signatures that declared themselves "required by law."

On the last day he brought documents to the counter,

Ángel carefully watched the official's every move. He watched as the man opened a drawer, pulled out a sturdy piece of card emblazoned with the emblem of the Peruvian army, wrote a few sentences in blue ink, and made a polite grunt while staring at the floor. Finally, he handed Ángel the voluntary military discharge certificate.

"Thank you," Ángel said.

He had now left the army. That afternoon, as he stepped out of the building, he saw cars hurtling along the avenue in a joyous frenzy. He thought he should climb into one of them and be free. He bounded down the steps two at a time. He felt the urge to say it again: he had left the army. He felt like going to a restaurant, raising a glass, and tucking into a *lomo saltado*, ideally with a fried egg on top, although he did not know who he could share it with.

That night, in a restaurant in Miraflores, he sat down and ordered several dishes. He was sitting in the middle of the restaurant, amid the bustle of people coming and going. He was served by a tall waitress with short, black hair. She had a checked apron, a wasp waist, and the impish expression of a little girl. As he gave her his order, Ángel asked with an awkward smile whether the waitress would sit and eat with him. She shook her head, but when Ángel paid and left an unusually generous tip, he noticed that she gave him a broad smile as she said goodbye. That was enough for him. This smile from a stranger was celebration enough for the evening.

"I never understood why you joined the army," his brother Daniel had often said. "But I'm glad you didn't die in the attempt. I can't imagine what it must have been like to be up in the mountains when the Shining Path were waging their guerrilla war."

On one such occasion, Ángel had found the words he wanted to say:

"I enlisted when Mamá died, you know that. What happened later just happened. I was recruited and I was posted to Ayacucho. It didn't seem so bad at the time. You already know why I was at that particular barracks."

On that day he was lunching with Daniel and his wife, Marissa, at their house. A photograph of their mother had pride of place in the dining room. Daniel's children, Vanessa and Jorge, popped in now and then to ask their uncle what it was like, being a soldier. He told them he would write a book about it someday.

"But how did you get out of there alive?" Daniel asked, when they were alone.

"I do my best to forget, *hermano*, that's the truth. But sometimes I talk to Mamá about it. She knows everything."

"You talk to Mamá?"

"I've got a photo of her, you know that."

"Sure, you're a little bit crazy, but that's not exactly news to us. When you're crazy, the most important thing is to admit it, the rest comes later. What are you planning to do with yourself now?"

"We're all crazy," Ángel said. "If you're not crazy, nothing makes sense. You already know that, *hermanito*."

That night, they hugged as they said goodbye. Ángel felt a sincere surge of affection for his brother, something he found a little strange.

His brother Daniel had always been first in his class. Being the big brother, he had assumed the burden of virtues their parents wanted to leave to the world. Ángel had always felt that he fell short. When they were at secondary school, Ángel gave up trying to compete with Daniel. Later, he made sure he attended a different university. His brother had studied engineering at the Universidad Nacional de Ingeniería, while Ángel had studied law at Universidad de San Marcos.

Neither ended up practicing his profession. Daniel ran a transport company, always arriving in the office at 7 a.m. to prevent another employee getting there before him. Ángel sold glassware and crockery in a shop near Surquillo market. Daniel would sometimes say that the best thing about a transport company was that the microbuses were constantly running. He always had somewhere to go. Ángel, on the other hand, led a quiet life, spending his days sitting in the store.

Daniel was elegant: he kept his hair cropped short, wore dark colors, and managed his family and his company with the firm hand of a driver on the road. Ángel was slightly chubby, and spent little time worrying about what to wear in the morning or what the rest of his day, or his life, would be like.

Daniel married a woman who shared his passion for order. Marissa was meticulous and obliging, and a lovely girl, something that had always worked in Ángel's favor: Marissa regularly invited her brother-in-law to lunch, inquired about his health, and gave him a little advice on how to soothe his aches and pains. She brought in money doing alterations and dressmaking for private clients. Daniel and Marissa had a house in Jesús Marpia, near Campo de Marte, and their children went to a good school. Everything was good with them.

Some years had passed since Ángel had retired from the army.

Truth be told, he had not had a bad time. He lived a calm life, adapting to his routines in the most original way he could.

Things in the country had improved since Abimael Guzmán had been captured. Fears that Shining Path might one day capture Lima—decapitating bank managers, local politicians, and the scions of wealthy families on the Plaza de Armas—had long since faded. The leaders of Shining Path were behind bars and the political wing, which had once defended terrorism, had fallen silent (some had been executed by the same terrorists they defended). Although there were still a handful of guerrillas in the jungle, those parts of the country that had been worst affected—like Ayacucho—were now at peace. "The situation is now under control and we are moving into a new era in our country's history," one political leader said. As time passed, international retailers and shopping centers began to spring up in Peruvian cities. To all appearances, the past was behind them.

Ángel lived in a rented room near Arco de Surquillo. It was in a dilapidated building, with a security gate of thick black bars and rusty iron grilles on the windows. The walls were gradually being invaded by large patches of damp.

His furnishings amounted to a small table, two chairs (one of them almost useless), a coffee maker, a low bed with a striped bedcover, a small yellow-tiled bathroom, and a poster of Claudia Cardinale on the wall. Ángel had seen her only once, in a movie set in the Wild West, but it had been enough for him to put her there.

It was home enough for him. He found it difficult keeping things tidy. There's nothing worse than a
mutiny by your belongings, someone had once said to
him. Papers, books, glasses, pens. If you leave them for
even a few days, they start an uprising. They move about,
jumble themselves up, slowly invade tables, wardrobes,
floors, silently threatening to evict the person who lives
there.

The bed was comfortable enough for him to get a
good night's sleep, despite the rattle of old pipes and the
banging of neighbors slamming doors. He woke every
morning at 6:00 and tried to leave as quickly as he could.
Once a month, he took a bus to the bank to withdraw his
pension.

One morning he saw a slim woman with long, silken
hair boarding the bus. He watched as she took the seat
in front of him. On the journey, Ángel gently touched
a strand of her hair as it swayed in the breeze from the
open window.

That afternoon, it occurred to him that loneliness
was like being adrift on a tall-masted ship that had lost
its anchor. On nights when he did not go to the fights,
the most audacious feat of the day, the one that required
real bravery, was switching off the television and finding
himself suddenly alone, in an unwelcome silence filled
only by the thrumming of the walls.

The first thing he did every morning was take the photograph of his mother from beneath his pillow. Good
morning, Señora. I hope you're well.

Ángel usually took a cold shower and immediately
afterwards, while his skin was still firm and taut, he had
breakfast in Surquillo market. It was his favorite moment

of the day. His friend Tania would always be waiting, ready to say good morning and serve him black coffee, papaya juice, and a piece of bread with queso fresco; he did not like to change his order. What he did like was seeing Tania and saying hello. Sometimes he even thought that she liked seeing him.

After breakfast, he went to the store where he worked as a salesman.

He was usually the one who raised the shutters in the morning. The store sold crockery and glassware, as well as plastic buckets, coffee makers, and brooms of every kind. He had gotten the job shortly after leaving the army and had no complaints. The owner, Señor Alana, told him he had been able to tell at a glance that he was an honest man. He would be working with Don Paco, who had been a salesman there for years.

By now, Ángel had been working there for some time. He was used to it. Waiting, selling, making small talk. He and Don Paco got along well and would take turns dealing with customers. Just being in the store, surrounded by shiny objects: there was nothing better.

"You never get bored," Don Paco said on his first day. "You get all kinds of people in here. And we've got something for everyone. You never get bored, take my word for it. Selling's not an easy job, but a broad smile is a big help. And I like smiling."

There was no door, just a large metal shutter, and the store opened directly onto the street, opposite the Zanjón and the flower stall. To either side of the entrance, they put small towers of plastic buckets. Inside were pots and pans, and at the back were padded shelves of tumblers, jars, and wineglasses. Ángel's worst nightmare was that an earthquake would one day bring the whole store crashing down around him and that he would drown in a sea of broken glass. But all the merchandise was top quality, this was what he always told the customers, and the glasses were cheaper if you bought them by the dozen. Better to die beneath a landslide of top-quality products than cheap tat, he thought.

Over the years he worked there he had become accustomed, almost addicted, to waiting on customers. He enjoyed his job because it allowed him to study the faces of the people who came in. The moment he spotted a customer coming in, he tried to guess what they did in their spare time, how many children they had, what time they got up in the morning. It was a game. From time to time, he enjoyed a fleeting encounter with an attractive woman. Between customers, he sometimes had time to read novels.

Since his brother had bought him a secondhand Toyota station wagon, he was also able to take special orders and deliver the glasses and crockery if the customer wanted. We're here to serve, he would say. I can deliver it to your door for only twenty soles extra. A lot of people did ask him to deliver, and in this way he got to visit unfamiliar neighborhoods.

He had managed to keep a pistol from his army days, and he kept it the glove compartment of the station wagon. Just in case a thief was interested in the glassware and crockery he was carrying. It was also a matter of personal security, he sometimes told himself. But he had never used it in the city.

Every morning he woke with the conviction that he was running out of time. It was a feeling that he was not completely present, that there was something missing in the air, something he could not explain. Images flooded

back to him. It was as though, every now and then, life
sent a messenger with a sign that read: "This is the past."

On this particular morning, the first thing he heard was
a gravelly voice before the radio news bulletin. It was
an optimistic message. Do a good deed today. Listen to
your heart. This was followed by an advertisement for
an academy that prepared students for college. *If it's college you're aiming for, the academia de Guerra can help you
score*, intoned the hoarse voice.

From the window of his room, Ángel could see the
leaves of a gently swaying tree down on the street. He
watched the leaves drop, one by one, like fallen angels,
full of grace. He saw two small black birds alighting on a
branch, twisting this way and that. A miniature paradise
that would last only a few moments.

He arrived at the store at 8 a.m. as usual, said hello to Don
Paco, who was already waiting, and sat down next to him.

At 9 a.m., he went to deliver pots and pans to an
address near the Plaza de Lince. He set off down the
Paseo de la República Expressway, and without knowing
why, he suddenly started to accelerate. A noise, a scream,
a freezing night, cars driving in circles, the images
whirled around him.

He had arrived at the end of the expressway. He did
not know when he had stopped. He suddenly found
himself in downtown Lima, in front of the monument to
Miguel Grau. He had to make his delivery. He could not
afford to be like this.

He arrived at the agreed-upon address, made his delivery,
and was given an envelope with money inside. When he

got back to the car, he sat for a while. His legs ached. He felt like burying his head beneath the steering wheel.

"We'll keep on keeping on in fits and starts," he said, turning the key in the ignition.

It was a phrase he often said aloud. He didn't really know what it meant but he liked it. The rumble of the engine calmed him.

The journey back was much shorter than he expected. He felt free, as though he were flying in the car. To any man in Lima, the most glorious sight is a street with no traffic. This is the supreme joy, a series of traffic lights that are all green, so that you can keep on driving until your time runs out.

To cap it all off, that morning he managed to find a parking space right outside the store. He went inside, put the money in the safe, and sat down next to Don Paco.

"Who's taking lunch first today?" he asked.

"You go ahead."

At one o'clock, Ángel went for lunch at the little café in the market. On weekends, if he had a little money to spare, he ordered fish with beans or *ají de gallina*. But on weekdays, he usually ate something cheaper, often *causa*, some rice with lentils, and a glass of passionfruit juice.

He bought a newspaper and walked past the line of carts piled with avocados, corncobs, and artichokes. When he came to the corner, he sat down at a white plastic table.

"Good afternoon, Don Ángel," said Tania.

"Today, I'll have a pork stew, *hijita*," he said, to her surprise.

That day Tania had tied her hair in a ponytail. As always, her eyes were shining, her movements quick and gentle, her smile dazzling. On several occasions Ángel had considered inviting her to see a movie. He had become used to seeing her here. Sometimes, as he paid her, he thought about brushing against Tania's fingers, so that he could feel another person's skin, so that that feeling might last until night.

Ángel leafed through the newspaper, reading up on the current corruption cases, until a bowl of steaming stew was set down in front of him. He ate a few spoonfuls of *mote* and pieces of tender meat. Then stopped. He needed to let it cool.

When he had finished, he ordered a coffee with milk, unaware that his life was about to change.

He finished it in three gulps, gave the newspaper to Tania, left ten *soles* on the table, said goodbye, and headed back to the store. He passed Don Paco walking the other way.

"I'm off for some lunch now. It's my only surprise of the day. Let's see what's on the menu," he said.

Ángel sat at the counter, flicking through the newspaper. He glanced through the sports pages. Then he switched on the radio. The words of a song told him that someone was going to love someone for the rest of their life.

No one came into the shop in the next half hour. This was worrying, because a store similar to theirs had just opened on the next street. They also sold glasses, cookware, and buckets. Worse still, they offered better prices and some customers preferred them.

Suddenly a beam of light fell on the tiled floor. The sun had come out, somewhat unexpectedly. Ángel turned off the radio. A silence descended, as though the sidewalk, the street, the traffic, all were very far away.

Then he realized that there was a woman in the store.

He had not seen her come in. She was standing very close to him.

She was a slender woman of uncertain age. Her long, black hair fell about her shoulders. She was wearing a dark dress that came down to her knees, that stood out against the pool of light on the floor. She had angular features, and her hands were clasped over her belly.

Ángel shuddered.

The woman stepped to one side. She was looking at the glasses. She picked one up. Her long red nails clasped the stem.

Ángel could not take his eyes off her. He felt a profound dizziness course through his body. It was as though the ground had opened up and he was falling into an abyss.

The woman picked up one glass and examined it, then another. Her sharply defined profile, her low, black shoes, a desolate hand touching her dress. She did not seem to be focusing on the glass she was holding, but on something far away.

There was no doubt: it was her.

She had appeared from the past, with her black dress and her slender figure, it was her. Her hair was longer, unsurprisingly, and her face was clean, but in her eyes there was a pale glint that he recognized.

Having seen her on so many nights, he did not find it difficult to recognize her.

Suddenly, the woman turned to him. She had just picked up another glass and was holding one in each hand.

"Good afternoon," she said, looking at him. "Can you help me?"

Ángel was trembling.

"Yes," he managed.

"The thing is, I want to buy a hundred of these glasses. But I need to know how much it would cost. Could you give me a discount if I buy a hundred?"

As her voice reached him, he felt a jolt of electricity.

Ángel barely moved his lips.

"Yes," he said.

"They're for a church group," she said. "We organize events for people in the neighborhood."

After a moment's silence, Ángel explained everything in a faltering voice. All of the glassware was made of tempered glass. He told her the prices of the various types and said that, if she bought a hundred, he could offer a 15 percent discount. He could pack them up and deliver them wherever she wanted.

He fell silent. He was trembling.

"That's great, thank you," said the woman. "I'll take a hundred."

She set the glasses back on the shelf.

"What name should I put on the receipt?" Ángel asked.

She gave him the name of a parish community. She took out a red leather wallet.

"Would you like me to pack them up? If you like, I can deliver them in the car. . . . It's a service we offer."

He paused. She looked at him.

"Would that be all right?" she asked with a smile.

"Like I said," he insisted, "I can deliver them wherever you want."

"I'll pay you half now and the other half when we get there," she said. "How much do you charge for delivery?"

It was the same voice. Yes. The same voice, he was certain now.

Ángel bowed his head. Suddenly, he could not bear to look at her.

The pen spun around in his hand.

At that moment, Don Paco reappeared.

"I didn't enjoy my lunch today," he said, "but what can you do, you've got to eat something."

Ángel was still looking at the woman.

"Twenty *soles*. I'll deliver the order myself. . . . You can come with me, and you can show me the way."

He did not know why, but he felt certain she had not come in her own car.

The woman looked straight at him. Her eyes were expressionless. Like a doll's eyes.

"That's fine."

"You stay here, Don Paco," he said. "I'll just make this delivery, and I'll be right back."

Paco was smiling. There was a crossword puzzle on the counter in front of him. His pen was moving constantly.

"I'll be right here," he said. "Don't worry."

Ángel packed the glasses into boxes as quickly as he could. The glasses rang like drums.

He carried the boxes to the station wagon parked just outside the store. He opened the back and carefully slid the boxes inside. The woman stood, watching him. Ramrod straight, motionless.

At last, everything was packed away. Ángel climbed in the car and took out his keys. The woman decided to take the backseat.

He heard a whisper.

The woman was getting into the car.

Yes, there she was. He could see her out of the corner

of his eye. In the rearview mirror, he could see a mane of hair. And part of her cheek.

For a moment Ángel's hands froze on the steering wheel. She was saying something: we're heading to Calle Alipio Ponce, Señor, it's in San Juan de Miraflores. Somewhere behind them, a car honked its horn and the woman began whispering again. She was suggesting the route he could take: if you do a U-turn here, you can get onto the Avenida Benavides, and then you just turn right.

She looked like a ghost, the black clothes, the stiff body, the taut thread of her voice as she repeated an address. Ángel did not answer. She gave him the name of the street again. Alipio Poncc.

The buses to his left were racing like a stampede of horses galloping toward death while he was moving forward against the current. The road ahead of him was clear as far as the bridge.

But Ángel had a strange feeling. It seemed as though the car was still stationary. He was not moving and yet, at times, when he accelerated, he seemed to move backward.

Perhaps it had something to do with the situation.

The customer in the back of his car was the same woman he had shot and seen fall dead. She was the corpse he had left behind one icy morning, years ago, on a dirt road near the barracks. But she had come back and now he was driving her somewhere.

Ángel thought about turning on the radio or singing something. Anything so as not to have to endure the silence coming from the backseat.

Still the woman did not speak. He could not help glancing at her from time to time. He saw a pair of black, impatient eyes that seemed as though they could see great distances.

He was familiar with the neighborhood where they were headed. He did not need directions. But just to hear her voice again, just to be sure, he asked the best way to get there. I already told you, she said, you take Avenida Benavides, go right to the end and then turn on to the Panamericana. From there, she knew a shortcut. This was the quickest way.

Ángel kept driving. The woman's hair fluttered in the gusts of wind but her face remained utterly still. She seemed to be gazing at something far away. Sometimes it seemed as though she were staring at nothing. As though gazing into herself.

Then, in the rearview mirror he saw her lean toward him. She studied him for a few seconds.

"Can you drive a little faster, please? I need to get these delivered as soon as possible."

Ángel saw her dip into her handbag. Rummaging through everything inside.

Had she recognized him? Had she remembered something? Maybe she was looking for a gun.

She bowed her head. Her fingers tightly gripped something inside the bag. Ángel could not see her clearly.

Just before the end of Avenida Benavides, they got into a traffic jam. The two of them sat, completely still. She held her hand to her temple, as though in pain.

Suddenly the line of cars began to move. Ángel moved into the lane to turn onto the Panamericana.

He was considering saying something. Then he heard her voice again, like a barrage of stones flying through the air.

"I'm running late, Señor. Drive faster, for God's sake."

After taking the off-ramp and crossing the bridge, they had to stop several times for traffic lights and at intersections.

At some point, she closed her eyes. Long eyelids, slender hands, between her brows a cross-shaped wrinkle. He could see part of her ear and a black dangling earring.

"It's very cold today, isn't it?" Ángel said.

He instantly regretted having spoken. It was a preposterous thing to say. A question to which there was no possible response. He should not have said it. Besides, it was better if she did not hear him speak. It was not a good idea to let her hear his voice. She might remember the edge of the dirt road, remember her body lying there, bleeding out, on that dark afternoon as she pleaded for her children. There was every chance she might remember. And she might remember the other thing. Above all, the other thing.

The woman did not move. Perhaps she had not heard him.

Should he say something else? No. He should not have spoken, should not have said a word, she might remember his voice.

Even as the car juddered along the road, a kind of inner gravity kept Ángel rooted to his seat. He had been clutching the steering wheel, but now and then he looked at her in the rearview mirror. She was still gazing out the window.

Then, suddenly, Ángel felt he should stop the car, get out of here, leave this place, run away, escape, flee, as though the weight of something, a physical weight, had settled on his shoulders.

But up ahead was a series of green traffic lights. Suddenly all the cars seemed to have shaken off some

burden, in a wild burst of madness, like a battalion of
soldiers launching an assault. He floored the accelerator
and drove as fast as he could toward his destination.

They arrived at the address. It was on a street lined with
small trees and a few flowering shrubs. The houses had
black railings and along the sidewalk were three rusty
iron posts. They passed a building with a large sign:
"Bodega-restaurant." They came to a blue building with
a crucifix mounted on the façade—a house that served as
a local place of worship.

"This is it," she said.

Ángel climbed out and opened the door to the trunk.
He started to unload the boxes of glasses. He carried
them into the house. Inside, was a table, a few pieces of
furniture, and religious sayings on the walls. With the
Love of God You Are Strong and Free. Do Not Suffer.
Have Faith in Jesus.

The woman handed him a banknote and murmured:
"Thank you." He nodded, bowed his head, and walked
back to the car. He sat motionless in the driver's seat.
After a while, he watched her come out again.

She had delivered the glasses to the house, and Ángel
assumed she was now heading home.

He could see her from behind. She moved with the
quick grace of a gazelle, her long, weightless legs barely
touching the ground. Her hair rippled in the wind. In the
distance, he could hear the rumble of engines.

Ángel watched as she took keys from her bag and
stopped in front of a house with a small garden, a block
from the house where he had left her. It was a small white
building; the windows were protected by iron grilles.
Blue geraniums peeked from between the bars.

The woman opened the front door. Then she vanished.

Ángel stayed in his car, unmoving. The day was cold, but a few lukewarm shafts of light fell across the road. He was trembling.

The first thing you remember is the cold. Your hands cracked and chapped, frozen solid from sentry duty, when you wake, you already know, but you have to pick up your rifle anyway, a soldier never puts down his weapon, you know that, compadre. Inside the bunkhouse, adobe walls, crossed beams, straw, everyone huddles together in the cold, it is the burning deep in your flesh, deep down, until a night comes, a night when you cannot sleep, not even for a moment. There is a guy there, a soldier everyone calls Sergeant Centurion, he specializes in torture. From time to time, prisoners are brought here, the patrol leader always says, here's a bunch of sons of bitches, but the women are sent directly to the captain, that's for sure, and the rest go directly to Sergeant Centurion.

Centurion was addicted to stringing up prisoners, connecting them to wires so he could watch their bodies jerk from the electric shocks. His friend, the comandante, was the same. That was Comandante Baquedón, the guy who once had the villagers of Santiago de Pischa and Ticlla dragged out to the square, do you remember? He marched them to the ravine and gunned them down, looking them in the eye, with not a trace of disgust. One bullet each, no need for waste, he said. He did it slowly so he could relish each one. There are a number of things you learn when you join the army. Inspectors are your allies, they're there to serve you, but it's important to be prepared for their inspections. Before an inspection, the

only thing to do is kill the women who have been raped
so that the inspectors can confirm they found nobody at
the barracks. Some of the women are reserved for us, for
the officers—but not all of them. The prettiest women
are reserved for the captain. You know this already,
Ángel, the reason you enlisted was because, after your
mother died, you couldn't feel anything, and so rather
than carrying on working at the school, since you could
no longer teach, better to come up here, to the mountains, to the cold, where you could try to kill a few terrorists, and to kill yourself in the process, as your brother
puts it. Up here, the cold and the fear, they make you feel
alive, compadre, they make you feel that you are not to
blame for what happened to your mother, that you did
not forget to visit, forget to give her her pills, up here is
a different world, and the best thing you can do is eat
whatever is slopped in your mess tin, and cut the throats
of a few peasant farmers—if they're terrorists so much
the better—all this so that you do not feel the fear. Let
these people come back and kill you, if they can.

    That's just how it is. In the morning you go out march-
ing, you go out singing, you go out shouting. You sing,
you march, you shout, and you eat so you can carry on
doing the same things. You're in a squadron, your fear is
such that it splits your skin from inside all day long. You
have to patrol the villages, see what is going on, then sentry duty, lunch, the search parties in the mountains, and
at night, the ice and everything that comes with darkness, Ángel. You'd already said you were going to join
the army, to stay there, with your friend Percy Huarón,
but Percy was shot right there, just after you arrived,
died while out wandering through the woods, picked
off by a sniper from Shining Path, but there is no time

to think about them, about the dead, there's no time to think about them, you knew that when you first got here, when someone dies, you have to pray for him once and then forget him, fuck him, remember? The dead quickly disappear into the past. The past is like hell; no one ever gets out.

Later, you'd go on the maneuvers, go on recess, but you were always terrified of being ambushed. A cold shudder you could feel in your skin, your bones, even on your prick. Often, the terrorists traitorously killed from behind, that was the worst, many soldiers died that way, and the terrorists would leave notes pinned to the corpses, this is what happens to informers, this is what happens to government lackeys, they'd slice off ears, cut out tongues and leave the bleeding body parts lying around, or stuff them in the corpse's mouth, with a trickle of blood to moisten the lips.

It had happened to some of the soldiers he ate breakfast with. In the morning, a soldier would pass him sugar for his coffee and by afternoon he would be dead with a sign around his neck: "This is what happens to government lackeys." And so it went on until you felt so embedded in the mountain cold, the dirty cold of mornings spent staring at the straw roof, at the hard, cloudless sky, the sultry moon of the night sky like a curse taking shape above your head, you were here to atone for something, you were here for this, for the prisoners, the sound of their heads slamming against the wall, the electric shocks to their balls, for a prisoner tied to a tree to see who could shoot him between the eyes. Fuck. You carried on firing long after he was dead, aiming for his head just to see the blood spurt, to have fun, to forget, thinking about this dead guy and nothing else. Thinking that if he was dead, you were alive. And the darkness and the silence of the stars and the farmers watching you arrive and the lambs left on the church steps. The steps leading up to the village church, and the woman and her mother, there they were.

Suddenly it was daylight again. He was sitting in his car, there was no one in the street.

Ángel got out. He looked at the church hall where they had delivered the glasses. It was right next to the house she had just gone into.

Would it seem suspicious if he went in and asked about her?

He did not dare, not then. He saw the sign saying "Bodega-restaurant." He walked in. He shuddered. She might be in here.

A few wooden tables, a counter with sweets and fizzy drinks and a Sacred Heart shrine illuminated by an electric candle. The table was lopsided and there was a crack in the top.

He sat on a plastic chair. The waiter came over. He had a broad, fierce nose with a pockmark on one side. He stared at Ángel as though from a great distance.

When Ángel was writing out the invoice, the woman had told him the name of the parish. He did not know her name. But he felt as though he had always known her. How could he find out about her?

Ángel ordered black coffee and plucked up the courage to ask the waiter a question.

"Señor."

"Yes, what can I do for you?"

Ángel raised his hand.

"The woman who lives on the corner, in the white

house with the geraniums," he said, "Do you know her name?"

The waiter glanced at the road, then turned back. He stared at Ángel.

"No, Señor, I don't."

"She never comes in here? She lives so close."

The man seemed disconcerted.

"Who is she?"

"She's slim, she has long hair. She helps out at the church on the corner."

The waiter stared at the floor.

"No, Señor. We've never seen her in here. I'll bring your coffee."

Ángel sat, staring through the window at the door of the white house as though she might appear at any moment. Should he go and knock on the door?

But the worst thing that happened up there, believe me this is the God's honest truth, the worst thing was what happened to the woman. So many years have passed and I have never forgotten. I can't forget. The wind whipping though the barracks that afternoon was bitterly cold, you can't imagine. I'd been on high alert all day; it had been raining and I was sure I'd seen men prowling near the perimeter fence.

This is what happened.

In the early hours, prisoners had been brought in from nearby villages. Soldiers routinely raided houses and rounded up people. They brought them in for inter-rogation and later killed them, so they couldn't tell any-one what they had seen. The soldiers didn't care whether these people were members of the Shining Path or not. That's just how it was, I'm not going to lie.

The simple fact was that the prisoners were locals, they were from Ayacucho, they were mountain folk, and that in itself made them suspects. By morning, the prisoners were gathered in a room. Some had started pounding on the corrugated iron, banging and screaming to be let out. The soldiers would go in and beat them. They dragged a few to the water tank and held their heads under. They had raped and murdered some of the women. That's just how things were.

On this particular morning, Ángel had seen a woman being brought into the barracks; she had long hair that fell to her shoulders. She was just another prisoner. But he had felt something quiver in his chest. From the moment he saw her, he had wanted to get closer. Had wanted to help her. But he could do nothing but sit and listen to what was being done to her. Then, when he could not bear to listen anymore, he had run away.

When he showed up again several hours later, a soldier came up to him.

"The captain wants a word," he said to Ángel.

Ángel got to his feet and looked at the shack that served as a barracks. As he stepped inside, the captain was writing something.

"You wanted me," he said.

The captain looked up.

"You disappeared for hours."

"I can't bear to watch what they're doing here. I can't."

The captain studied him.

"Better get used to it, soldier. You should have been there today."

"Sorry."

The captain nodded toward the wall, to a pile of burlap sacks. The corpses were inside.

"Well, I'll let it slide this time, but do me a favor. Take these to the roadside and leave them there. You know how it works."

Ángel looked at the five sacks, then turned to the captain. Yes, sir, captain. I'll take them right now. He moved slowly, lifting the sacks one by one and loading them into the back of a truck. They were heavy. He closed his eyes as he loaded them.

"They're all dead," the captain said, still writing something. "But if you see anything move, shoot it. Keep an eye on the girl in the top sack. If she moves, shoot her, you know the drill."

The captain gestured to one of the sacks Ángel had already loaded. It was stained black, Ángel did not know why. He finished loading the truck.

He started the engine with a roar. He pulled away.

Ángel drove along the stone track. The blue-black sky was slashed by the jagged line of mountain peaks. He pulled up by a gorge next to the road.

This was the usual spot. This was where the truck came to pick up corpses. It was important to make sure they left no trace.

Ángel lowered the tailgate and started to unload the sacks. There were three men and two women, he realized. The woman he had seen arrive was one of them. Their features were still visible through the burlap. He turned away as he dragged them from the truck. He could not bring himself to look at their faces.

"I'm sorry, I'm sorry," he said to them, feeling utterly ridiculous. What was he doing, asking them for forgiveness, what was he doing talking to them? Yet he felt he had to say it. The dark sky clouded over. He could see the line of bundles, the features just visible through the burlap. His final task was to recover the sacks, since they would be needed for other bodies.

At the moment, he saw the farthest sack moving. Suddenly, a face appeared. The face of the woman. That woman he had seen arrive.

He watched her sit up. She tried to struggle to her feet. She fell back. But then she managed to extricate herself from the sack. She was standing, her long dress ripped, shreds of skin hanging off her bones, her face bloody, her voice no more than broken sobs and screams. Ángel watched as she moved her hand, then her head. He could make out a few words.

"Please," she said. "Help me. My children. I have to find my children. Please."

Suddenly, the woman stopped.

"You know me," she said.

Ángel took a step back.

"Please," she insisted.

Then Ángel's hands reached for his rifle. They were his hands, but it felt as though they were acting of their own volition.

He was scarcely aware of what he was doing. He shouldered the rifle, aimed at the woman, and pulled the trigger. She crumpled to the ground. He took a few steps back and ran to the truck. With a grunt, he hauled himself into the driver's seat.

Ángel drove back to the barracks at breakneck speed, the tires sending up clouds of dust.

He had shot her, she had crumpled. Her tear-stained face had said: "Please. Help me. My children. I have to find my children." He had shot her and left her behind.

But he had not left her behind. She had come back. This was the woman who had come into his store that morning to buy glasses. The same woman who had sat in the back of his car, given him the address, disappeared into a house in San Juan de Miraflores. He could see her now, through the whorls of steam rising from his coffee, hear her voice pleading with him to find her children.

Ángel drove back, past houses, buses, and telegraph posts moving in reverse.

As he reached the Avenida Tomás Marsano, driving down an empty road, he suddenly stopped. He turned the car around and drove back the way he had just come until he finally reached the San Juan de Miraflores. He parked in front of the house he had seen her go into. Was she still there?

He would sit for a while and wait for her.

He turned on the radio, listened to a beer commercial, then changed the station. A couple of long howls and then the same beer commercial. He saw some boys walking slowly. Were they neighbors, did they know the woman, did they know her name? He wished he could ask them. He envied them. They were close to her. He wanted to see her, to touch her.

He ran his hands across his face several times. He felt better, as though he had wrested something from his body.

The urgent need to see her again was like a lightning bolt inside his body. He wanted to say something to her. He needed to know that she was all right. To help her in some way he could not define. To ask her how she had escaped. That was all. He didn't want to bother her. He just wanted to know.

"I got stuck in traffic," he said as he went into the store.

Don Paco studied him. He knew Ángel was lying, but the long years of working together had made him tolerant, something Ángel appreciated.

"Traffic can be a bitch," Don Paco said sympathetically.

Ángel served a number of customers that afternoon. He packed boxes, took payments, gave change. He stored the takings in the safe. The owner would come to collect it at six. It had been a good day.

Just before he closed up, he took out the photograph and talked to his mother.

"I saw her today. The girl I told you about."

That night Ángel decided he needed to take a walk around the neighborhood. He could not go back to his room. He would go to the park in Miraflores and watch the people, wander around, sit on a bench, lose himself among the trees, remember. First and foremost, remember.

He wanted to somehow dispel these images yet still keep hold of them. He saw cats prowling between the flowers, they stopped and stared at him with their glowing eyes. They knew.

And *you* know only too well. You are there, look again, I know I've said it again and again, but it feels good to say it, the creeping cold beneath the skin, the pale terror of the moon, the fitful sleep on bare floors, the grit on your teeth, your gums. I heard it from Palacios, the cholo. The smell of garbage, of flesh, of piss, the black acrid smoke that burst forth from her skin. For anyone who was there, it is the stench of charred flesh that lingers longest, that smell of damp fire.

A head leaning against the iron bars, wires attached

to the woman's breasts, her hair disheveled, her eyes, yes, those dark, sunken sockets staring as the soldiers hook a battery to the cables that will make that body jerk, a joyous shriek of sizzling: the gray flare, the first scream, the stink of a crippled leg. When they switch on the current to the cables, the white howl of that night, that hour that is still going on. That night had been memorable, because they had assumed this woman would not be able to hold out like the others, but, for a time, she had surprised them, she had endured, her eyes squeezed shut, without a scream, without a word, until she was completely paralyzed. That's what they told him. Sergeant Centurion had finished the job and now the captain was giving orders. That was when the captain told him to keep an eye on the girl in the top sack. If she moves, shoot her. You know the drill.

Then he had carried her out to the truck, taken her to the roadside. But as he dragged her by the arms and dumped her there, he felt something overwhelm his heart. Then he noticed the sack moving, and then it happened. She had struggled to her feet, wrapped in her tattered dress, she had stood before him, her arms wide, her long hair splattered with blood. She had pleaded with him, and having no idea how to answer, what to do, he had shot her.

"I'm sorry," he said now as he sat in the park in Miraflores, his legs stretched out in front of him, while gray cats, sausage vendors, and lovestruck couples strolled around. A gust of wind stung his eyes. He watched a police van drive past. Soon, the other truck would drive past. The soldiers would collect her body, take her to the river or to the furnace, make her disappear without a trace. Just then, a gently calm breeze was drifting through the park, stirring the mass of trees, the flowers, the absentminded passersby. A sandwich vendor in a red and white uniform was going around handing little packages to people nearby. But shortly before she had said something, had spoken to him, I know you, why did you do this to me, I know you, we used to be together, don't you remember, back when we were kids. Had she said this?

Ángel sat on a bench. Given all the dead bodies he had seen, why could he not shake off this image? This woman who was almost a corpse, the shreds of skin hanging from her bones, this was something that he and the others had done, that they had done to her. How had she managed to survive? Her skin striped with purple welts, her elbows grazed and bleeding, a gunshot and him leaving her atop a pile of bodies, but she had once been a part of his life, she had said so. "I know you." He hadn't answered, perhaps he had known her once but he could not remember when. Only now did he realize that this was what she had said. And in the moment before Ángel shot her, the woman who had come to his store that afternoon had said something more. "My children," she had said. "I need to find my children," as she clutched her chest.

There was a constant hum of traffic. Black exhaust clouds belched from the cars. Ángel passed the Café Haití, stopped a moment, saw groups of people laughing. They all looked so happy in there. His legs ached.

It took him a while to get home. He went up to his room, opened a cupboard, and took out a bottle of rum.

The room had created an internal silence, as though immune to all the sounds coming through the window.

He filled the glass and savored the harsh tang of the liquor. He turned on the television just to be sure there was one other living person in the world. It was a game show. Which jungle fruit is yellow and has the smallest seeds, you've got forty seconds, starting NOW! Somebody gave the answer. The audience applauded. The presenter said something, but it wasn't his voice.

The following day, Ángel woke feeling as though he had been on a long journey. He turned on the stove, heated the coffee, raced down the stairs, and ran into the corner store. He felt like eating breakfast alone. He headed back to his room with a banana and a *chancay* roll. The sweetness of the bread was comforting.

He turned on the television and finished his breakfast. He arrived at work early.

At noon, rather than going for lunch, he went to his brother's office.

He found Daniel sitting at his desk reading the newspaper. Just seeing him made Ángel feel better.

Daniel was always well turned out, with his neatly pressed jacket, his sober, polished shoes, those thoughtful eyes that revealed his generous nature. Daniel was an exemplary brother, always garrulous and proactive, an immense force for good in an unstable, shifting universe.

"You all right?"

"Yes. Why do you ask?"

Daniel folded the newspaper. His phone rang; he immediately picked it up and said, "Yes, that's fine." Then he looked at Ángel, his ear still glued to the receiver.

"Because you look like shit."

"I didn't come here for you to insult me."

Daniel put a hand over the receiver.

"I'm not trying to insult you, I'm telling the truth."

Daniel added, "That's fine, we'll go with that," and hung up the phone.

"So, what's been happening?"

Ángel felt a twinge in his throat.

"Nothing. I'll come see you some other time. I can see you're busy. I'm sorry."

Ángel left the office. He could feel his brother's eyes boring into his back.

The following day he woke up late. It was his day off. He did not have to go to the store.

It was almost ten o'clock. Through the window over-looking the Calle Leoncio Prado, he saw Doña Adelaida, who had a stall selling *anticuchos*. Her apron was like a uniform: the stains and patches were like medals, decorations that attested to a life of hard work. She had already fired up her grill. A line of skewers threaded with chunks of meat gave off a soft crackle.

Ángel went outside and sat on a nearby bench, where he spent a while chatting with Doña Adelaida and the few customers who stopped to buy. The meat tasted like soft earth and she was a little heavy-handed with the *ají*, but it was edible.

In the afternoon, he went to the hospital. He waited for the elevator, walked down endless corridors, and came to the room. It was here that the captain, his former boss, had been for months.

Sitting on a chair, wearing a pair of dirty pajamas, the captain's eyes were vacant, staring. Ángel remained standing. He briefly considered saluting.

"Morning, boss. Or rather good afternoon."

The captain sat watching him.

"You don't need to talk. He can't understand," said the nurse standing next to him.

Ángel glanced at her, then turned back to the captain.

"Just so you know," she said.

By the time he left, it was already dark.

He headed home, took another shower, and dug out a sweatshirt, a T-shirt, and a pair of shorts. He packed his bag. Put on a coat.

He glanced at his watch.

Back out on the street, he turned this way and that. He saw telegraph posts lined up in the mist. He realized he was sweating. Or perhaps it was the drizzle.

At nine, he stopped off at a restaurant called El Pollo de Oro and tucked into half a chicken and fries. The chicken seemed particularly delicious that night. He felt the surge of energy he always had when he was about to wrestle. When he finished eating, he gulped down a cup of black coffee. He climbed into the car. Negotiated the narrow corridor of streetlights and shadows. He came to the street with the large gate. This was his night in the ring.

He feels his skin prickle on those nights in Chorrillos, the dirt floor, the makeshift tent of guy ropes and stakes, next to the Cancha de los Muertos. It is almost ten o'clock and people are packed into the bleachers to watch the *luchadores* walk out.

Ángel walks between the broken boards, feels a sharp stone underfoot. The wind whips at the canvas.

The roar of the crowd, the glare of the lights. In one corner, a slow, scrawny man with a pockmarked face is selling candy bars and sodas from a tray.

Around the canvas, the air is thick with yellowish dust. A ramshackle wrestling ring, a dented fight cage.

In the distant glare, two shadows are wrestling, Saurio Manco and Taita Mena. Two aging, flabby men in wide, baggy shorts circling each other, fists jabbing in the half-light. They look like crazed chickens flapping their wings as they run in circles. Bathed in an ashen glow.

Around them, the monsters lined up on the bleachers roar, they laugh, they hurl stones that bounce off the wire cage. A sea of contorted faces who flock here from various barrios throughout the city on a Friday night.

More monsters slowly file into the tent, like an army of ants devouring a corpse. They do not come alone, always in groups of four, of five, of ten. Sometimes they arrive shouting or singing, "Luz, luz para mis ojos." The clamor of voices rises in a chorus, marked by a drumbeat, as they take their seats in the stands. There the monsters assemble, half-open shirts, garish shoes, tattoos of butterflies and scorpions. Still they sing, stopping only now and then to bellow, "Kill him, kill the son of a bitch." Roars of laughter, cheekbones, red sneakers, gobs of spittle, wet mouths, monsters pouring into the stands, a fetid, sweltering mass.

Ángel went into a little room that served as a dressing area. There was a toilet, a window, a small table, and a chair. On the way, he passed John—El Gordo—who had already begun to sweat, who stared at him with vampiric eyes.

El Gordo owned the place. He had been a wrestler and had taken his many defeats in the ring with good humor. "The more punches you throw, the more the money mounts up. That's always the way," he would say. Ears like sweaty, malevolent wings sprouted on either side of a face zigzagged with scars. His face gave him the necessary authority to send wrestlers into the fight cage, to take the entry fees and the bets. "Here, men fight for honor," he would say. "To be the best." This motto was how he justified keeping most of the winnings.

El Gordo followed Ángel into the changing room.

"You're up next. Get a move on."

Ángel rubbed a little cream onto his body.

Outside the fight raged. The referee had not shown up that night, but Saurio and Taita had agreed on a few ground rules. Step into the ring, roar and grunt, stare each other down. They had made a pact: no blows below the belt. A wrestler had once kicked another in the balls and had been permanently barred on the orders of El Gordo.

To see that his rules were enforced, El Gordo had two assistants, El Cabo Gutarra and El Zapallo Reina. El Cabo was poker-faced, thin and tense. He wore wire-rimmed glasses with grimy lenses that helped him see the world more clearly. His job was to keep the dressing room tidy, but in fact he spent most of his time inventing stories to encourage the fighters to hit harder. El Zapallo, "the Queen," on the other hand, was smiling and fawning, spellbound by the bodies of the wrestlers. His eyes shone as he raised his arm to signal the beginning and end of each round. With El Zapallo and El Cabo in attendance, the fights would continue.

The ring was illuminated by a couple of floodlights mounted on black poles. The fighters dodged and weaved to avoid their opponent's punches and to avoid being blinded by the spotlights.

Through a gap in the curtains, Ángel watched the fight. The wrestlers were locked in a clinch, as though they were lovers. Suddenly it happened. Taita head-butted Saurio and knocked him down. Saurio lay sprawled on the sweat-stained canvas. From his eyebrow came a trickle of red. El Gordo stopped the fight.

A sullen young man climbed in to hose down the canvas.

"You're up," El Gordo said.

Ángel stepped into the fight cage and watched his opponent make his entrance. He was pitted against Zambo Samson, a thickset, thuggish man whose punch no longer had the power it once had. The paunch he had acquired through many nights drinking beer forced his body forward. Zambo's chest and arms were covered with old scars, the result of years spent robbing banks. Even so, Ángel could not feel confident. His opponent glared at him. Zambo still had enough bitterness in his soul to throw a good punch.

Ángel felt a nervous pleasure. At that moment Samson looked like a black bison about to charge. Ángel began by circling him, like a fly, trying to find a gap where he could land a punch. His footwork might throw his opponent off for a while. Every time Ángel managed to sidestep, he lashed out with all his strength. The punches boomed out in the air. But Zambo barely registered them.

Ángel managed to land several punches on his opponent's face, only to suddenly receive a powerful blow that left him stunned. He was surprised to find himself on the canvas, his elbows aching and an acrid taste in his mouth. He struggled to his feet.

When the bell sounded for the last round, he felt relieved. He had lost, but he had held out to the end.

He was in less pain than he had expected.

Back in the dressing room, Zambo gave a few guttural

grunts by way of apology and uttered the usual phrase: "A job is a job and a punch is a punch, compadre."

Pressing an ice pack to his face, Ángel watched as people streamed out of the venue. They all had somewhere to go, a house, a bar, a brothel.

"Goodbye, maestro," he said to John.

El Gordo peered at him with his black eyes.

"Go on, get out, and try and hang on to the few hairs you've got left."

It was midnight when he opened the door to his room. He took another shower and looked at the photograph of his mother. Then his eyes fell on the photo of the captain he had long kept.

I lost today, captain. But like you always said, you have to carry on. And I carry on so I can talk to you. Tell you what I'm thinking, the things I couldn't tell you back then: tell you how much I still hate you, captain. That's why I keep you here with me, just so you know. Because we haven't finished our conversation, you and I. We're not done. That's all I'm saying. I never thought . . .

He trailed off. He took a few steps and slumped onto the bed. He would not sleep yet, but he would try to get some rest, find a little peace on the edges of the pillow.

"Easy, now," said a voice from the photograph. "You know you need your sleep. And here you are. No need to think about the woman now."

Ángel got up and stared out the window. His body felt as though it might burst. He could feel a fire raging inside him. Outside, far beyond these houses, was her face, and her voice: my children, I have to find my children.

Then he saw something in the sky. The crude, white, tarnished circle of the moon. There it was. Tonight, the moon had broken free of the clouds obscuring it, and shone, alone and happy. It was a solid mass that gave off its own breeze. Ángel could feel the moonlight coursing beneath his skin, like new blood in the darkness.

It was a message. Ángel thought he was a fortunate man.

Lady Luck had been good to him, it had sent this woman back again.

He paced his room, went back to the window.

Find her, talk to her, say what he needed to say. It was a mission entrusted to him by fate.

He had not had the best life, he thought, but it had its comforts. To be able to lie down on a bed, stare at a ceiling when he was alone, sing in a low voice, talk to himself, earn enough to eat *anticucho* now and then, imagine he was surrounded by the verdant hills, like when his mother was alive, when they lived up there.

But a new idea suddenly opened up before him. A life unveiled by his apparition. He should leave her in peace, but he also needed to say something to her, or to hear her say something. He had found her, now he had to speak to her. This was his chance.

If she told him, I'm fine, I'm at peace with what happened, if he could hear her say something like that . . . you shot me, you left a wound, but I'm not dead. I got up and I walked away. A family found me, they saved me.

Was it impossible? Could he hope to hear such a thing?

Suddenly, he saw the moon. Perfectly clear. The voice.

II

The following morning, he got up, quickly undressed, and got in the shower.

He scrubbed himself with the towel. He felt as though he was late for a meeting.

It was 7 a.m. when he pulled up outside the woman's house. The white façade, the blue geraniums, Calle Alipio Ponce.

To his surprise he did not have to wait long. The door slowly opened and there she stood.

Yes, it was definitely her. She set off down the sidewalk with long, determined strides.

Long hair that fell about her like a veil, a black skirt that fell to her knees, a pair of low-heeled shoes. But there was someone with her. She was leading a little girl with a blue schoolbag, a checkered blazer, and a cap. The girl clutched her hand tightly, struggling to keep up.

They reached the end of the block. The woman quickly looked both ways. Ángel watched as she took out a bunch of keys. She was opening the door to a house two blocks from her own. The brick front was painted black. Ángel heard the sound of the door closing.

He sat motionless in the car, with the engine idling. He suddenly realized that someone behind him was honking their horn. It was a taxi driver with a face as long as a fiddle in a white car that looked like an ambulance. Ángel pulled away. He pressed his foot on the accelerator.

Later that day, when he left the store, he headed back

to his place, near the Plaza de Jirón Inca in Surquillo. The carpenter on the corner had taken his planks into the street and was sawing a sheet of plywood. A warm breeze swirled around the walls. Next to him, the small trees swayed. A lady in a black dress walked past, clutching her throat.

Ángel went into a local bar. Wooden tables, chairs cobbled from lengths of timber, the floor littered with sawdust. A few shelves lined with dusty bottles.

Ángel sat down and ran his hand several times over the plastic tablecloth. The waiter brought a bottle and a glass.

Ángel poured out the beer, watched the bubbles eddy, and took a sip. The liquid continued to swirl as the wooden table rocked.

A group of men was sitting nearby.

"See that little prick?" he heard one of them say. "What d'you think he's looking at?"

He longed for the men to come over. It would have given him great pleasure to break one of their noses.

The voices became hushed. Then there came a murmur and a roar of laughter.

Ángel continued to take little sips. He pictured the face of the woman as she clutched the little girl's hand.

He drained the bottle.

The beer had left a bitter taste. He felt himself enter into a state of silence.

The men at the next table talked in loud voices, but he felt very far away from what was happening all around. He stared at the bubbles at the bottom of his glass.

He should take his mother's advice. Not see her again. Let her take her own path. The path that he had left her on that night. After all, what was he to do with her? So many people had died in Ayacucho during those years. No one would remember her, or blame him or call him to account. He should go home. Keep working at the shop, tallying the day's takings and giving them to the owner, eating hominy soup for lunch, having a breakfast of *chancay*, coffee, or soda with Tania, lining his body with a little fat and his pockets with a little money, visiting his brother from time to time, talking to his photographs. Such was his life during the day. And some nights, to undo what had come before, he would stuff his gear into his sports bag and head for the ring to smash some bastard's face or wait for someone to smash his. It wasn't the best life, but it was his, and it wasn't the worst, all things considered. There was no need to change it running after some woman who had returned.

That night he sleeps badly, then well, then badly again. At daybreak, he leaps out of bed and heads for the bathroom.

He goes to the store and tells Paco he has to go see his brother about something urgent. He will come straight back.

Shortly afterward, he arrives at his brother's house.

It is 8 a.m., when Daniel is usually reading the newspapers over his second cup of coffee—the only time, he claims, that he truly enjoys.

Ángel finds him at the kitchen table.

"Hi, Ángel. Fancy a coffee?"
"No. Not right now. Thanks."
"Sure. So, what's up?"
"You remember I told you once about a woman? A

woman up at the barracks. How afterwards I dumped her on top of a pile of corpses."

"Yeah, it rings a bell. But that was a long time ago. I thought you'd forgotten about all that stuff."

"There's something I never told you about her."

Daniel sipped his coffee.

"I don't know why you keep going on about it. You've already told me this story a bunch of times. You sure you don't want a coffee?"

"No, thanks."

"Up to you."

Ángel settled himself in a chair, rubbed his face, and looked at his brother.

"I was responsible for transporting her body. But . . ."

"You were in a pretty fucked-up situation. You were just obeying orders."

"But she regained consciousness and suddenly there she was, talking to me. I could barely hear her."

Daniel looked at him.

"And?"

Ángel turned the glass between his fingers.

"She said we knew each other. She begged me to look for her children. Then I shot her, but you know that part."

Ángel's words hung in the air between them.

Daniel rubbed his eyes, then looked at his brother.

They sat in silence. Ángel was not sure whether his brother was exasperated or whether he simply had no idea what to say.

Suddenly Vanessa and Jorge, his niece and nephew, appeared. They both smiled as they repeated his name. Ángel hugged them. I thought you'd be at school by now, how are things? We're fine, uncle. But you should come visit more often. We never get to see you these days.

His sister-in-law, Marissa, came into the kitchen: she was as slim as ever, with close-cropped hair and a smile that lit up her whole face. Ángel got to his feet and kissed her on the cheek.

"Hi, how are you? I'm just off to run some errands for my mother, Danny. I'll see you later. *Chau*, Angelito."

After Marissa and the children left, there was an abrupt silence.

"What were you saying?"

"I was telling you about the woman. The one from that night in Ayacucho."

"What about her?"

"I saw her the other day."

"What?"

"She came into the store."

Daniel took a sip of coffee. There came the sound of a car hurtling past at top speed. The windows rattled.

"You sure it was her?"

"Yes, I'm sure."

"And did she recognize you?"

"I don't know. I don't think so. She didn't say anything. But since I saw her, I've gone back to her place a couple of times looking for her."

Ángel got up and poured himself another glass of water. He sat down. A sparrow alighted on the windowsill.

"Why did you do that?"

"What?"

"Go back to her house. Don't do that."

A passing bus set off a car alarm. The wail continued for some time.

"I'd been thinking about that night and I never realized. All this time."

"Look, it's a nightmare, but don't let yourself get caught up in this thing. At least you know you didn't kill her."

"To be honest, I don't know what's worse."

"It's a horrible situation, but there's nothing we can do about it now. It all happened a long time ago. Life goes on, *hermano*."

Daniel offering advice was a habit. Ángel was grateful for it, through sometimes he found it infuriating.

"I thought she was dead, Daniel. I thought I'd killed her."

Ángel had raised his voice.

Daniel sat, motionless.

"I don't understand why you keep tormenting yourself. What good does it do?"

"It was something I did."

"I know."

"She stood there, almost naked, her clothes ripped to shreds. And then—I don't know—she started moving. I was half crazy myself. I'd been boozing all day. I'd drink so I didn't have to see what the other guys were doing. I found myself thinking all sorts of things. I thought someone might show up at any moment and kill us all. You know? But the captain ordered me to transport the bodies. And then, all of a sudden, she got up and started talking to me, and I shot her."

"But . . ."

"I don't know what happened. I went mad. I thought I might die at any minute. And I shot her, just like they ordered me to."

Daniel said nothing. A wisp of steam rose from his cup.

"Ángel, I don't think you're capable of doing

something like that. I think you imagined it. You couldn't have done something like that."

"But I did."

"I'm not convinced. What you're saying to me sounds impossible. You're not like that. In any case, what happened, happened. There's nothing to be done about it now. What are you going to do?"

Ángel felt like pounding his fist on the table.

"I don't know. This story has been haunting me. That's what's so fucking ridiculous, Daniel. She's always there. It's like I can hear her again. I feel like she's talking to me again."

Daniel stood up and put on his jacket.

"Shit, you've been fucked in the head ever since you got back from that place. But it's all in the past now, you moron. Look, I'm going to say it again: they arrested Abimael Guzmán, have you got that? The war's been over for a long time now. There's no terrorism these days. It'll soon be a new year. We have to get over it. We can't carry on brooding about that shit."

"It wasn't my choice that what happened, happened," Ángel said as he got to his feet.

Daniel looked at him calmly.

"I'm going to say something I should have said before," he said, dropping his voice to a whisper. "The truth is, I think you were really brave to take up a post in Ayacucho, *hermano*, to fight. I've got a lot of respect for the things you did."

Ángel took a step back. He smiled.

"I don't want you to respect the things I'm telling you about," he said. "I don't want you to admire them or whatever."

"So what do you want?"

"I don't know. I don't want you to give a shit."

A bird landed on a branch near the window. It seemed to be peering inside, looking for something to eat.

"All right."

"I want to tell you how I feel, I want you to listen, and I want you to not give a shit."

Daniel put an arm around his brother's shoulder and walked him to the door.

"Listen, Ángel. I'm going to tell you something. This Saturday we're throwing a party, it's Marissa's birthday. You'll get to meet Jacky—she's pretty, I think you'll like her."

"Yeah, I've met her, I remember."

"Thing is, she's crazy about you. That's what Marissa told me. Said she's crazy about you. So . . . we'll be expecting you on Saturday."

"I know I have to carry on."

Daniel slapped his brother on the back.

"Look, I don't know what else to say. We're here. We're alive. We might as well make the most of it. As much as we can, anyway."

"Don't worry."

Daniel opened the door.

"So, don't forget," he said, raising a finger. "Don't be a moron—we'll be expecting you at the party on Saturday."

There was a long silence. They looked at one another.

"Okay. And thanks."

As he was leaving, Ángel heard Daniel's voice again.

"Promise you won't go back to that woman's house. The truth is, you were lucky. You could have died up in Ayacucho. You have to let this go."

"I know."

"Be grateful that at least you're still alive. Promise me you won't go back there."

He stepped out onto the street. He could still hear his brother's voice. Of course. He was right. Be grateful that you're still alive. At least.

When he got back to the store, Paco was waiting. It had been a slow morning, and they sat talking. Paco had been a professional soccer player for a while, then a taxi driver, then he had enlisted, and then he had been a driver with the Municipal Transport Company. He was widowed and now lived with his daughter. He talked about these different stages of his life in the same way. He was about to turn seventy.

"I have done a bit of everything," he said. "And I'll carry on doing a bit of everything. I've never been particularly talented at anything. That's why I've had a quiet life. Not being particularly good at anything and living a quiet life is what I like best. And besides, someday soon I'll pass away peacefully. That's something I'll be good at, you'll see, I won't whine or complain or anything."

Just then, an elderly woman came into the store and started inspecting some of the cookware sets. Her eyes were green, her skin dotted with freckles, and her shoulder-length white hair was cut in a very harsh line.

"I'm interested in buying some pans," she said. "But I need quite a few. Someone told me that you can deliver. Would that be possible?"

"The car is parked right outside," Ángel said.

The woman checked the prices, examined the bottom of the pans, and said she would take four sets. They were for a popular restaurant in Villa El Salvador.

Ángel carried the boxes out to the station wagon.

He started the engine.

He barely spoke to the woman as they drove. When they reached their destination, he took the payment and set off back toward Lima. The highway was empty.

Suddenly, he saw a sign for an exit ramp. He took the exit. There it was. Calle Alipio Ponce.

He pulled up close to the house. This was better. No one could see him from here. There was a newsstand on the corner. He got out, bought a newspaper, and went back to the car. He leafed through the pages.

He saw the church hall where they had dropped off the delivery that first day. He got out of the car and walked toward the door, his legs moving of their own volition.

He was greeted by a smiling, friendly nun.

"Excuse me," he said. "I'm looking for a young woman I came here with a few days ago when I was making a delivery."

The nun looked him up and down.

"Would you like a catechism?" she said. "They're cheap, only five *soles*."

"No, thanks. It's just that I'm looking for a woman . . . Don't worry, it doesn't matter."

Ángel turned and went back to his car.

Over and over he told himself that he did not want to bother her. He simply wanted to make sure she was all right. To see her appear, go to the house next door, come back. That was all.

He was parked in front of the white house, the one he had seen her go into.

As he read the newspaper, he heard voices on the radio. The year was coming to an end. Listeners called in to talk about their hopes for the new year. The presenter cracked a few jokes and time passed.

Ángel allowed himself to be distracted by the voices. There was a commercial break, then a news bulletin, then a song. He was simultaneously listening and reading.

Suddenly, near the corner of a page of his newspaper, he saw her appear. She was wearing black pants and a blue blouse, and her hair hung loose around her shoulders.

She was holding a little girl by the hand.

Without thinking twice, he climbed out of the car.

He stopped in front of her. At first the woman did not notice him. But he took a step forward.

"Excuse me."

The woman did not seem surprised; she and the girl walked past. Ángel followed and caught up to them. She quickened her step and he walked beside her.

"Excuse me, please. Don't you remember me? Can't you see me? My name is Ángel Serpa."

Without stopping, the woman turned. There was a deep furrow on her brow.

"What's wrong with you?"

"I'm . . ."

The woman walked more quickly. The girl almost had to run to keep up.

"I have no idea who you are, Señor. What's wrong with you?"

"You don't remember? You came into the store. And actually . . . you already knew me. I don't know what to do. I just want. . . . I'm sorry. I don't have . . ."

"What are you talking about, Señor? You're not making any sense."

The woman walked away. Ángel heard the pounding of her footsteps. He ran to catch up with her. She turned.

"It's just . . ."

"Please, leave me alone. What's the matter with you? A woman can't even walk down the street these days."

"I thought you were dead. But you're not . . ."

She carried on walking. The breeze created swift ripples across her blouse.

There was a man walking in the opposite direction. The woman walked faster and faster. She clutched the little girl's hand, forcing her to take longer and longer strides. Ángel knew that she had recognized him. She simply wanted to flee from him.

He walked behind her.

"You don't remember?" Ángel said, coming alongside her again.

"Remember what? Please, Señor. Leave me alone."

"I was a soldier up in Ayacucho. You begged me to look for your children. I shot you. You don't remember? I don't . . ."

The woman stopped. She looked him in the eye. An expressionless face, a fire raging beneath her skin, the liquid depths of her eyes.

Behind her, the road ran its course, the cars and pedestrians, the lofty telephone poles, a line of bowed trees. They were both standing, staring at each other, beneath the frozen sky, next to the mound of corpses.

"I just wanted to know if you're all right," he said.

She bowed her head, shaking it from side to side, then looked up at him. Then she simply stood, motionless.

Something in her forehead seemed to move, as though she had had a revelation.

"I don't know what you're talking about, Señor," she said.

"You don't remember?"

"Leave me alone, please."

The woman started walking again. The girl scurried to catch up.

"I just want to know, that's all."

"Please, go away."

Suddenly, he heard a voice.

"What's going on, Aunt Eliana? Who is this man?"

The girl stared at him.

"Don't worry," the woman said, squeezing the girl's hand. "Just come with me."

"Do you know him?"

"I don't want to bother you, honestly," Ángel said. "Could we meet up some day, just to talk? I want to know how you got through it. How you saved yourself. What it was like. You've no idea how happy I am that . . ."

"Please, Señor, we have nothing to talk about," she said.

There was a gust of wind. Out on the street, some boys were playing with a ball. The woman carried on walking, dragging the girl behind her.

"But . . ."

"I don't know who you are. If you don't leave, I'll call the police, Señor."

Suddenly she began to run toward the bus stop, her hair streaming behind her. A bus had pulled up at the corner. The girl scampered after her.

Ángel stood there. His back ached. He was alone on the street.

He could see the line of lampposts and shifting shadows.

The little girl had mentioned her name.

Eliana.

For some moments, Ángel did not move. At length, he slowly walked back to his car.

He put the key in the ignition. He would have to tell his mother about what had happened, he thought.

At noon, a group of tourists came into the store. They were tall, blond, and overweight, and they talked in loud voices. They had no desire to buy anything. They simply took photographs of the pots and pans, the prices and the glasses. In a few days, they would all be back with their families in Washington or Copenhagen or London. They would show off their photos at some social event and explain: a market store in Lima, buses on the street, barrowloads of fruit, pots and glasses hanging from wires. Look! One of the tourists picked up a pan, set it on his head like a hat, said something unintelligible, and the others laughed.

It was at that moment that Ángel made a decision.

After the tourists left, there was a long silence.

The afternoon passed; a few customers came in to look around and ask for something or other.

Shortly before six, Ángel got to his feet.

"I'm heading out for a while," he said to Don Paco.

"No problem, I'll close up," he replied.

Ángel got into the car. His route was clearly marked on the windscreen. The honking car horns led him to San Juan de Miraflores. It was as though his hands were refusing to be guided by his body.

He had decided to change tack. It had been a mistake to confront the woman, he thought. He needed to find out a little more about her. What she did, whether she worked, whether she was a member of the religious community that met in the house down the street. Did she live alone or with family? He needed to know everything.

He turned into the street. There was the door. The white façade, the wooden shutters, the small patch of garden, the blue geraniums. On the corner, an empty parking space was waiting for him.

He parked the car, jumped out onto the sidewalk, bought a newspaper from the kiosk, and retraced his steps. He sat behind the steering wheel. He would wait here, read a little. People walked past and stared at him. From time to time he played some music, then turned it off again. He didn't want to run down the battery.

It was getting dark. He should leave.

Still he waited.

Then he saw her appear.

It was her. It was Eliana, and it was as though he were seeing her for the first time. There was an impulsiveness in her appearance: blue outfit, slender legs, long undulating hair. There was someone with her. It was a young woman, her hands clasped in front of her, holding a book that looked like a Bible.

Ángel started the car and drove slowly, following them at a distance.

He watched the two women walk along the road. They went into the building where he had delivered the glasses that first day.

As the door opened, Ángel heard music and voices. An elderly woman with gray hair came out to meet them. Inside, a group of people raised their arms in greeting. It looked like a party.

From his car, Ángel could still make out the sounds coming from the church hall. They were singing hymns. A few more people arrived.

Ángel stayed there, staring at the façade. A group of boys were kicking a soccer ball further down the road. A faint glow filtered through the door of the restaurant on the corner. From the windows of the church hall came the sound of hymns, then prayers, then more hymns.

The people coming to the place all wore jackets or suits.

Ángel got out of the car and walked slowly to the restaurant. He wanted to see what was happening inside the building, but someone had drawn the curtains. In the restaurant, he bought a can of beer. He went back to his seat.

It was dark now. He could hear the muffled roar of engines from the avenue.

Still the music carried on. Ángel had heard these hymns a long time ago, perhaps during his childhood. "Faithful son, I strive to love thee and to live for thee alone, to sing thy praises asking nothing but to die while praising thee." He had sung this hymn. But when?

The door opened. A group of people filed out. They were laughing.

Eliana was among them, at the end of the line. Her sharp profile, her long arms, the black locks falling over her shoulder. She was kissing the elderly lady, the one who had greeted her, on the cheek.

Ángel saw her step out onto the street.

Eliana had realized that he was there, he thought. She was weighing up her options, deciding whether to confront him, to call the police, or to just keep walking. Yes. She was deciding what she should do. For a split-second, he was convinced that Eliana was going to take a gun from her purse and shoot him. Still, he sat where he was. He watched as she arrived at her house. A light, the flash of a key, the dull thud of the closing door. A sense of emptiness, of the street pervaded by her form.

Ángel started the car. He would spend the night alone. With the photograph of his mother. And with Eliana.

He woke several times and always with Eliana's face next to his on the pillow.

He arrived early at the store. The sky was overcast, but the air was heavy and humid.

A few buyers turned up. Don Paco took charge of serving them while Ángel tallied the prices and took the payments. That afternoon the owner, Señor Ginés Alana, came to collect the takings.

That night he was scheduled to wrestle. This time his opponent was Killer Gómez, a man with a mane of hair and the curled mustache of a musketeer. Killer never set foot in the ring without half a bottle of rum inside him. He had the vacant eyes of a fish and a mouth that made small guttural sounds. Perhaps this was why El Zapallo Reina and El Cabo Gutarra worshipped him.

Ángel arrived at the arena, pulled on his shorts, and smeared his body with cream, rubbing it in with deft movements. The moment he stepped into the ring, he launched himself at Killer and managed to land a punch on the side of his face. He followed this with a flurry of punches. He punched him in the sides, feeling the man's resistance flagging. He dispatched his opponent in three rounds and the crowd roared. Long screams turned into howls and back to screams by the end. Ángel stood, panting for breath, next to the body of his victim. El Zapallo came over to bring Killer around and take him away. He would look after him.

That night, Ángel made a little money. His eye was swollen, but with some ice and maybe a chunk of raw steak it would be fine.

He arrived home in the early hours of the morning. He pressed ice to the swelling, took a painkiller, and slept soundly.

The following morning he pulled up outside the house on the Calle Alipio Ponce at the time when the woman usually took the girl to school.

He saw the door open. Eliana appeared. Her head held high, a long gray dress, the girl in her school uniform: a pinafore and a blouse.

He walked to the corner, unsure of what to do. Go up to her, say something? He didn't know what to say. But that didn't matter. He was prepared for her to insult him, to slap him.

In a sudden burst of daring, he walked up to her.

When he came close, he saw her turn to him.

Her black hair, her smooth forehead, and the two vertical, immutable lines of her cheekbones. Her motionless pearl earrings, like seeds.

She was stiff, bolt upright, one hand extended, the other holding the girl.

"Señor, you ... for God's sake. I don't believe it. What's happened to your face? For God's sake, just go."

"I want to give you something."

"Who are you, Señor?"

Ángel realized he was gripping her arm. She wrenched it free.

"Let go of me. What's wrong with you?"

For a moment, he saw that same look of terror. He stepped back.

"My name is Ángel. I was a soldier up there, an officer. But I never wanted ... I ... you don't remember? You begged me to look for your children. And I did something terrible to you. But listen. Please. Here ..."

Ángel took out the money he had won at the fight the night before, the banknotes neatly packed into a grubby white envelope. The woman carried on walking. But the girl was staring at Ángel.

Eliana was walking away as quickly as she could. There was a police officer nearby. Ángel watched as she walked over to him, then pointed at Ángel.

"That man is harassing me," she said. "I don't know what's wrong with him."

The officer strolled over slowly. He had bushy sideburns, the eyes of a toad, a large mole near his mouth.

"Listen, you," the officer said. "You leave the young lady alone."

Suddenly a shadow appeared. A masculine figure. It had emerged from a house on the same street. The man was walking quickly toward him. The figure gradually grew brighter until it stopped and then was bathed in light.

It was a man about fifty, his hair disheveled, his eyes boring into Ángel.

Ángel saw the man's apelike expression, exaggerated by the dark features.

"What the hell is wrong with you? Why are you pestering my daughter?"

He stood there in front of Ángel, breathing heavily.

"No, honestly, I didn't mean to pester her. It's personal."

"Personal . . . ? I'm her father. Get out of here. Go on, get out."

Ángel stepped to one side. A car raced past.

The officer stepped closer.

"Don't worry, *jefe*," the man said, "I'll deal with him."

The policeman shrugged.

"I don't want any trouble here," he said.

"I'm sorry, I didn't mean to upset anyone," Ángel said.

An ice cream seller had stopped his three-wheeled cart and was staring at them. His eyes were small and hard; he seemed prepared to intervene.

"Get out of here," said the man who claimed to be Eliana's father. "You leave her alone. She's my daughter, I won't have anyone bothering her. Am I making myself clear?"

Ángel took a step back.

"Go on, get out of here," the man said.

Ángel remained on the street. All of a sudden, he was alone. He stood for a long moment, trying to keep his balance, pitting his will against that of the man's by not retreating. Then he forgot what had just happened. For a moment he had no idea where he was.

A family was clustered around a car parked on the corner. The door opened. A mother was helping her child get into the car.

Eliana and the man who claimed to be her father had vanished.

Ángel saw the bodega. What the hell, he thought.

He went inside. From behind the counter, a woman with a wrinkled face looked at him. She was wearing a white apron and smiling.

He ordered a beer and the woman served him immediately.

"Thanks."

Ángel looked at the woman. He made small talk about the weather. He ordered another beer.

"With pleasure," she said.

"Can I ask you something, Señora? Do you know a

woman who lives around here, she takes a little girl to school? I think her name is Eliana."

Ángel poured the beer into his glass without looking at her. He sensed the woman pointing toward the door.

"Oh yes, that's Señorita Eliana. She takes her niece to school every morning. A good woman, she is."

"Eliana? Do you know her last name?"

"I don't. She sometimes comes in here to buy things."

"But you don't know her surname?"

"No, Señor. The family's name is Huarón, I think. I'm not sure. Would you like some crackers?"

"Yes, please."

The woman went to rummage through the shelves.

Ángel sipped from his glass. The bubbles rose slowly and burst as they reached the surface. He had found something out.

The woman named Eliana came from another house to visit her niece. And her last name might be Huarón.

But why had she pretended not to remember him, to not remember what had happened? She had probably recognized him but wanted nothing to do with him. That was hardly surprising. But he had to persevere. Now there was another obstacle to overcome. A violent man who claimed to be her father. Ángel needed to convince him that he meant no harm.

As he ate the crackers, Ángel noted down the name of the church hall on the corner. Then we wrote: "Eliana Huarón."

As soon as he got back to the store, he did a search for the religious center. He typed it into Google and then cross-referenced it with Eliana's name. The search produced no results.

That afternoon, he phoned Cholo Palacios. Though he had not seen him in a while, he often thought about Cholo.

They had been stationed together in Ayacucho, at the same barracks, and had spent nights chatting as they relieved each other on sentry duty.

Ángel remembered the nights of cold and fear they had spent together, desperately trying to decode every menacing sound, starting with every bird call. But it had not all been fighting. He and Cholo had hunted deer together, and had gathered a sweet fruit called *banadilla*. They had sampled the local delicacies: *sopa de chuño*, *patasca*, *puca picante*, sweet potato-and-pumpkin *mazamorra*. Having eaten them so often, they came to love these dishes. They had discovered a hatchery called Sol de Huamanga, with its multicolored birds: the parrots, the *tuya*, the kestrels. At night they heard the wings of owls hunting for blood. They had also seen prostitutes—known as "charlis"—showing up at the barracks.

Every morning, Ángel and Cholo did military exercises with the other soldiers: sometimes armed, sometimes unarmed. The cold prepares you for anything; running with your teeth clenched prepares you for what's in store.

The memory of the horrors they had both seen had created a bond between them. They had made each other promises about what they would do when they got out of there. On the day they arrived home, Lima looked like a new city. They had spent only a year in Ayacucho, but, looking at the broad avenues in the city center, they found them strange and beautiful.

Cholo was the only person Ángel knew during his time at the barracks with whom he kept in touch. Cholo worked in the Public Registry office. In the public records at his disposal, he had already tracked down some of the war veterans, many of whom had died in road accidents or from cancer. Others, unable to bear the memories, had taken their own lives. Cholo had told Ángel about many such cases.

Oh, and the other day someone came in asking about you, Cholo said. Who could it have been? Never mind, it doesn't matter. I need you to help me with something.

Cholo's voice on the phone was as cheerful as ever. They arranged to meet.

Ángel arrived at the office around lunchtime. The walls were hung with a calendar, a crucifix, and a few public service announcements. His friend was sitting at a desk. He had not changed since Ángel had last seen him. He was a thickset man, with a round face and tiny doll-like ears. His desk held a holder with some pencils, a notepad, and a dusty computer.

They hugged.

"Let's go get some ceviche," Cholo said.

"Sure," said Ángel. "But I have a huge favor I need to ask."

"What is it?"

"A name."

"Are you trying to trace someone?"

"I've got an address, I just want to know who lives there."

Sometime later, Cholo had the name of the man who owned the house where Eliana lived. The property belonged to Alfredo Domínguez, who was married to Otilia More.

"You can even see them if you want. There they are, husband and wife. Do you recognize them?"

"No. I've never seen them before. Isn't there a family called Huarón listed?"

"I don't see any mention of anyone called Huarón."

"What do the Domínguezes do?"

Cholo glanced at the screen.

"Nothing. They're dead. The Domínguez family. It says here they were civilian casualties in an attack by Shining Path. The incident was recorded in Vilcashuamán. That's all it says."

Ángel leaned forward again. A few brief sentences. Civilian casualties of Shining Path raid. Six words. This had been the end of their lives.

"Can you tell who's living at the address now?"

"A member of the family. Or maybe someone has rented the place. It's not listed."

"That's that then. I don't know what to do."

"If you want, there's a place in downtown Lima where you can check the names of those involved in cases up in Ayacucho. It's part of the Public Defender's Office."

"That's good. Have you got the address?"

"Ceviche first. Let's forget about this stuff for now, compadre."

They walked into the cevichería: wooden tables, plastic palm trees, and darting waitresses in blue blouses. They sat. The tablecloth was patterned in pastel triangles. Cholo said:

"Shit, you've stirred up so many memories of that time. Sometimes I don't know what to do."

"I don't talk to anyone else about it, but I talk to you."

"I don't want to remember anymore."

"But there's one woman I can't forget, Fortunita Quispe."

"Who was she?"

"She was a local. Someone found a red bandana, said she was a fucking terrorist. Zambo Guerra said she was a terrorist. I bet you remember what they did to her."

Cholo turned away.

"There are times when I can't get my head around such evil. It's something I just can't understand. Maybe it's a madness. Do you think that it's possible for a whole country to go crazy at the same time?"

They sat in silence.

"Back then, I refused to participate in the rapes," Cholo said at length. "And so did you."

"But I was ordered to dispose of the bodies and that's where I saw this woman."

"Which woman?"

"The one I'm looking for," Ángel said, raising his hand. "Something happened with her."

A skinny waitress with dark circles under her eyes walked past, muttering "Good afternoon, I'll be right with you."

"I thought you never did anything."

"That time, something happened. The captain told me to take the body and dump it somewhere it would be picked up. I thought she was dead. But suddenly she got up and started asking me about her children. Then I was confused, I didn't know what to do. I shot her and I left her there. I thought she died there. Ever since, I've been haunted by the fact that I killed her. But you'll never guess what's happened. I saw her a few days ago. I saw her. She walked into the store and asked to buy some glasses. I even delivered them for her."

Cholo's eyes were wide.

"You saw her? Did you tell her who you were?"

"Yeah."

"You told her who you were? Really?"

"But she says she knows nothing about it. I don't understand. If she doesn't want me to talk about it, I get that. Maybe that's why she's turned me away."

The waitress came over. Her face was careworn and covered with bruises that formed a kind of livid map, as though she was acquainted with men and their violent ways.

"A couple of beers, to start with," said Cholo.

Cholo glanced around, as though looking for someone. The place was full of diners.

"I've heard people are investigating all the stuff that went on up in Ayacucho. I have to tell you, that scares me."

"I don't feel scared anymore. In fact, I wish there was something I could do to feel that fear again."

A group of men sat down at the next table.

It was a large group, men wearing green polo shirts, all talking at the same time. From time to time they would roar with laughter. One of them was wearing boots. Ángel felt as though they were wearing uniforms.

The waiter brought their beers.

"Divine liquor to soothe the soul," Cholo said, raising his glass, "and we both know the soul needs soothing, compadre."

The following day, Ángel went into the city center, passed the Palacio de Torre Tagle, and found the office Cholo had mentioned. Located in the Commission for Human Rights, it was a small room with a single desk, two computers, and a set of thick three-ring binders with many pages. These contained dates, locations, a few details and incidents. A young woman asked to see his ID, noted something in a register, and told him he could use one of the computers.

He began searching. The woman's name might be Eliana Domínguez or Eliana More or Eliana Huarón. He could find no record for any of these. He searched for any woman whose first names was Eliana. There were eight, but all were either dead or lived far away. It was possible she had changed her name. But there were still some pages he could search through.

He decided that the best thing to do was head back to Cholo's office. He closed the archive folders and said goodbye to the receptionist. He drove through long lines of traffic belching fumes. Here and there, street hawkers hustled at the traffic lights.

He found Cholo in conversation with a tall man who had a hooked nose.

"There's no record of any Eliana," he said.

Cholo glanced at him, then said goodbye to the man.

"How hard have you looked?" Cholo leaned forward.

"This is the woman I'm trying to trace. Her name is Eliana. But I don't know where to find any information about her."

"So, what's the deal?"

"I already told you. I saw her. She came into the store. The woman I told you about, the one I left lying by the road. That thing I did . . ."

Cholo frowned. He seemed annoyed about something.

"And are you sure it's the same woman?"

"Yes. I want to find out where her family is. What happened to them."

"If she says she doesn't know you from Adam, maybe you should forget about it."

"It's not that easy, Cholo. I want to know what happened, how she got away from there, what's happened to her since. And maybe I want to help her, I don't know."

Just then, a gray-haired man wearing a suit came into the office. He was short and wiry with a nondescript voice that sounded like a recording. The man requested certain files. Cholo asked him for his ID, then rummaged through a drawer and handed over a folder. Without taking his eyes off Cholo, the man took the folder and went to sit at one of the desks.

"What you need to do is roughly calculate her age, and search for her using her name and date of birth. That way, you might end up spending years looking for her," he said, smiling, "but who cares?"

"It happened early in 1992, and she was very young at the time. But I can't be sure."

"You make things complicated, Angelito."

Ángel felt a burning anger well up in his throat.

"Don't fucking talk to me like that. I'm not complicating things, I'm just trying to find out who she is."

Cholo looked at him. The man leafing through the folder looked over and then returned to his reading.

"Don't be like that."

Ángel fell silent.

"Look, I just want you to understand."

"It's all right. Don't worry."

Ángel took his head in his hands.

"I'm sorry. I don't know what's wrong with me."

Cholo opened a drawer. Inside, there was a bottle.

"Let's go get a pisco or something. That way we won't overthink things. See what happens when you think too much, compadre?"

Thinking too much was a bad idea. Better not to think at all. Not to remember the things that had happened, the things they had done. Obviously. I've already told you, but I'll tell you again. Sometimes the soldiers would smear their bodies with the women's blood. They would daub themselves with blood and shout or sing. They would cut off the women's heads. They would take them to the morgue. They would put them in body bags. They would smear blood over their faces and sometimes their chests. On other days they would hold the men in one house and the women in another. They would rape the women, promise them that if they didn't struggle, their husbands would not be killed. He had seen it himself. In Cayara, in Hualla, in Tiquihua. And the images flooded back to him, more terrible than ever. A woman drenched in blood walking through a field in the sunshine. Yes, but for her, for Eliana, he could have . . . but not anymore. Because she had come back. She was there, standing in front of him.

They went to a bar near Cholo's office and knocked back glasses of pisco. The place was almost empty but it was noisy, with a dull roar like the rumbling of a water pump. They sat for a while, drinking and chatting.

"Right, I have to go," Ángel said, eventually. "I need to get a few hours' sleep."

"Why?"

"I've got a fight tonight."

Cholo refilled his glass. Took a sip.

"Shit, I don't know why you still do that."

"Because I enjoy it. We all have our little quirks. And mine is wrestling."

"Fair enough."

"Let's meet up again soon."

Ángel was silent for a moment.

"Thanks," he said. "And sorry."

"No problem. After all these years I know what you're like."

Ángel gazed at Cholo sitting in the chair. There he sat, just as he had a few years ago at the barracks.

That night Ángel arrives early at the wrestling ring. His sports bag feels lighter than usual. He goes into the changing room, strips off and stares at himself in the mirror. He is scared to see a line crossing his chest, like a wound foreseen.

He feels cold. He pulls on his shorts and sneakers and smears himself in oil. He does some jumping jacks. He needs to numb himself before going into the ring.

Tonight, he is scheduled to fight La Araña Negra— the Black Spider—who weighs in at ninety kilos and has beady insect eyes and rolls of fat that hang over his shorts. Ángel knows the guy well. He used to work as a security guard for a bank. These days his body is a wreck. He has to alternate his punches just to keep his balance.

In younger years, the Black Spider had his hour of glory when he racked up ten fights undefeated. Now, he dyes his hair black, bellows on his way to the ring, and walks with a slight limp. But his fists can still pack a punch.

At 10 p.m., Ángel is ready. The ache in his joints seem to have eased. He feels light. There are sporadic roars from the audience, the thud of sweaty bodies, the white glare of the canvas.

Ángel climbs into the ring and does some jumping jacks as he sizes up the Spider, who emerges, stony-faced, from the other side. There comes the crackle of the loud-speaker announcing their names. Then he is alone with the other man in a vast emptiness.

He sees the Spider raise his arms. His short, tensed body glistens with oil. Ángel bobs closer. He knows the odds are in the Spider's favor, but he thinks he can win if he keeps his distance and throws a punch whenever his rival lets his guard down. Then he hears a scream from somewhere in the darkness. He is not sure whether it has come from him or from up in the bleachers.

The Black Spider moves closer. Ángel spots a brief gap and jabs his fist into his opponent's ribs, an unexpected lunge. This breathing scrap of skin, this liquid mass that blinds him for a moment, this mass of flesh facing him. A glistening hulk, blinding patches of white shimmering on this oiled body. Bring him down, finish him off, destroy the mass in front of him. From somewhere deep in his gut, a wave of black fury surges through Ángel: he wants to see this pestilential mass explode, this sweating hulk shatter into a thousand pieces. His punches plow deep into the man's body and Ángel imagines a hole will open up and that he, too, will be swallowed up in the entrails. He can feel the clammy skin, can see it soaked with his tears and, with a howl, he lunges. Then pale eyes, a crunch of bones, a head crashing to the ground, a dull thud.

Ángel finds himself standing, alone. Around him, a scattered, dusty light. He sees the Black Spider sprawled on the canvas. Sees him writhing in pain. The Spider is dazed. But he struggles to his feet.

Ángel suddenly feels a strange energy. He rushes at the Spider, unloading all the pain contained within his hands, twisting his knuckles, laying waste to the viscous mass before him. In this moment, his only thought is of killing the man and then dying himself. Again and again he pounds, again and again. Eventually, something in that limp mass gives way, the Black Spider falters and collapses. Seeing him once more sprawled on the canvas, Ángel lashes out with his feet, feeling a fierce, insistent pleasure he has not felt in a long time. He stands, panting for breath, as his opponent's body writhes below him.

El Gordo opens the gate and rushes over to stop him, he grabs Ángel's hand, and holds it aloft. Ángel is the winner. In the stands, the monsters whoop and cheer, they leap to their feet as though this is an uprising. Someone blows a whistle. Those who have won their bets wave their arms.

Ángel slumps to the ground and lies there, next to the Spider's limp frame. He reaches out. He wants to shake his hand. He had not wanted to hurt him. He had simply needed to punch something. He is not sure what came over him. Thankfully his opponent gets to his feet, spits on him, then storms out of the ring and disappears into the tunnel.

The following morning Ángel wakes with pains in his arms and his mouth. Bruises have gradually blossomed on his cheeks. He sees light streaming through the window. He reaches for his wallet, checks how much he won. Puts the money in a hole behind the wardrobe.

He feels his body ache, but also the need to move. He could go out for a run right now.

He turns on the stove, drinks coffee from the white mug. He checks his wallet again, slips it into his pocket and heads off to the store.

Eight o'clock. All he has to do is wait for Don Paco

and the customers. Suddenly, he has a realization. It is astonishing. The pain from last night has vanished.

In the afternoon, he goes back to the Commission for Human Rights. He checks through some files on the computer.

A different woman is at the reception desk. She is slim, her piercing eyes staring at him through her glasses, and Ángel suddenly feels that she knows everything about him. She listens as Ángel explains that he is looking for information about a victim of the war in Ayacucho. Do you have a name? she asks.

The woman is slightly shocked by his bruised and battered face, but she hides it well. She sees me as a monster, Ángel thinks. That's what I am. People will run screaming when they see me coming. He silently thanks the woman when she comes over to his computer.

"Her name is Eliana and she was in the 'emergency zone' up in Ayacucho," he explains. "She would be about forty now. She might be going under one of three surnames."

The girl taps a few keys.

Eliana, you said. All right, let's see what we can find. What are the three surnames? Eliana Domínguez. Eliana More. Eliana Huarón. Nothing comes up.

Don't worry, Ángel says. I can keep searching. She leaves and he sits down in front of the screen.

He does not find anyone, but he will carry on searching. He remembers the approximate date. He finds a series of news stories from different years and different regions. None relate to the Eliana that he knows. He just wants to find out a little bit about her. That's all.

Someone comes into the office and asks for something.

Ángel carries on with his search, and after a series of interruptions and unintelligible names, the screen freezes. Time stands still

A photograph. Backlit by the screen.

Staring out at him, a motionless face in the black light. It is her.

He sees her.

Eliana María Cauti.

This is her name. This is her. Yes.

Her eyes and her hair and her skin. This is the woman he has seen so many times. The woman he dumped by a roadside in Ayacucho. The woman who crumpled when he shot her. The woman who came into the store at the Surquillo market to ask about the price of the glasses. The woman who walked near her house on Calle Alipio Ponce with a little girl who called her "*Tía* Eliana." This is her.

Ángel feels a chill course through his body. He is trembling, he tries to regain his composure but he sees his hand fluttering in the air. He clicks on a link.

There is an article. Eliana María Cauti. Torture victim. According to her witness statement, she was dumped with a pile of corpses by soldiers who assumed she was dead. She woke with a mouthful of irrigation water. According to the report, she scrambled down the hill and made it as far as a small farm, where she was found, unconscious, by a local woman who took her into her house and hid her for several days. Later, she appeared before the Truth and Reconciliation Commission to give evidence. She had lost her husband and her two children. Both of her parents had died in attacks by the Shining Path.

Eliana Cauti was treated by doctors. Then she

disappeared. Current whereabouts unknown. End of report.

It was not a good photograph, but there was no room for doubt. It had been taken from a public document or an identity card. It was just a photograph: the fixed gaze of someone posing for an official photo, giving no hint of the life within.

He noted a date of birth, in Ayacucho. Some general information, too. Nothing more.

He could work out what had happened afterward. Eliana had tracked down a brother or a sister in Lima. She had moved to San Juan Miraflores. She walked her niece to school, helped out at the local church hall. But one thing still did not make sense. According to the report, both of her parents were dead. So who was that man who said he was protecting her, who had threatened Ángel, who seemed to live there? Why had the man told Ángel not to upset "his daughter"?

Ángel took a few banknotes from his wallet. He rolled them up, stuffed them into an envelope, and set off for Eliana's house. He had no idea what exactly he would do. Perhaps he would just ring the doorbell, say "this is for Eliana," and leave. That would be best. She would understand, surely.

Night had drawn in. Ángel pulled up by the house, got out, and rang the doorbell. As he waited, he shifted his weight from one foot to the other. A man appeared on the street. He walked toward Ángel.

It was the same guy who had threatened him the day before. He was walking quickly toward him, a dark outline, his face distended.

"Señor. If I could just . . ."

"You again?"

"It's just . . ."

"I don't know what your problem is or what you're doing here. Just leave."

"I came to give something to Eliana, Señor."

"My daughter's not here. Just go."

The man stood, facing him. His eyes blazed.

Ángel put the money in his pocket and walked back to the car. He sat for a moment, hands on the steering wheel, before driving off. It was a broad avenue; he put his foot on the gas.

The following day he called Cholo Palacios. The name Eliana Cauti appeared in the Public Registry together with the same details he had found in the Ombudsman's Office. She had no known address.

After talking to Cholo, Ángel visited his brother's office. He found Daniel sitting at his desk.

The transport business was booming. They had bought new furniture. These days, they had filing cabinets and two desks with computers. There was a door leading to a courtyard where they parked the vehicles.

"What's with you? You're covered in bruises, what happened?"

"I won a fight."

"Oh . . . so you're still doing that shit. Do you get a kick out of spending your nights wrestling in that dump?"

"Yes."

"Oh, well . . . to each his own, I suppose. I don't know if you're a moron or a masochist or both."

"Enough with the insults, buddy."

Daniel smiled.

"Okay, okay, I'm sorry."

"I won and they gave me a bit of money. That's what I wanted."

"At the cost of your health? One of these days you could be knocked out permanently, *hermano*."

Ángel felt a surge of energy. It was true. His brother Daniel worried about him. He could see it in his eyes: a sparkle of affection and good-natured understanding. Why did it annoy him?

"I took the money to the girl."

"What?"

"I wanted to give her some money, Daniel. I wanted to give her something. But I ran into that guy again. He wouldn't let me."

"What guy?"

"The guy who claims to be her father. He threatens me whenever I go there."

"What the hell were you thinking, going there? Honestly, I don't understand you sometimes."

Ángel nodded, although not at what his brother was saying.

A secretary with curly hair came over to give her boss a document.

Daniel signed it and then turned back to Ángel.

"You want a coffee?"

Ángel looked at him.

"I know who she is now. I know her name."

His brother raised a finger.

"Have a coffee."

"Yeah. Thanks. I'm dead on my feet."

Daniel buzzed his secretary. "Two coffees and a couple of ham sandwiches, please, Norma." As he turned back to Ángel, his eyes welled with tears.

"You know you can't carry on like this. All you're going to do is destroy yourself."

"I don't care about that anymore, Daniel. I know who she is now. I know her name. Eliana Cauti."

"I don't understand why you need to know her name."

"I already told you, I want to help her."

A group of drivers came into the office, nodded to their boss, and headed for the bathroom. The tallest of them said something and all the others laughed. Ángel assumed the guy had said something about his appearance.

"Look at them," said Daniel. "They've been working most of the night, but here they are. This is the one business that never stops. Even on Sundays and in the middle of the night the microbuses keep running. We never stop. I like that."

"I can tell."

"Life is like the transport business, *hermano*. Apologies for the corny comparison."

The secretary appeared carrying a tray with two cups of coffee and two sandwiches. Slices of red onion peeked out from the edges of the bread. A few drops of oil dripped onto the plates.

Ángel and Daniel had eaten breakfast together since they were children. They could eat in silence, they felt no need to talk, like people who were comfortable with each another.

From the window came a constant hum of traffic. Around them, telephones rang and the secretary answered each call with the words "Serpa Transport."

"Anyway, as I was saying . . ."

"One question first. . . . Tell me something. How do you think this obsession with her is going to end?" Daniel asked, passing the sugar.

Ángel stared into his cup. The coffee danced from one side to the other, reflecting the ceiling lights and his face. It was a miniature storm.

"I want to know she's all right, although I know that's

not much. Actually, I'm doing it for myself, so I can feel better too."

His brother bowed his head and stirred his coffee. The telephone rang, but he barely moved. He carried on staring.

"All right," he said. "I suppose that's . . ."

"I don't know what to do. I don't know what to do with this memory."

"Try to forget it, Ángel. And come to the party on Saturday."

"I can't."

He had spoken more loudly than he intended.

There was a silence.

"You can't come?" Daniel said.

Someone in the next room answered the phone.

"But I'm grateful, honestly."

Ángel sipped his coffee, which tasted watery and bitter. He added a few more spoons of sugar.

"Take it easy with the sugar."

Ángel pushed his coffee to one side.

"Listen, I'm going to forget this whole thing, like you said. I'm going to leave that woman in peace. I've done enough damage already," he said. "Besides . . . you know. What happened, well . . ."

"You'll never change," his brother interrupted.

"You don't know me."

"I've known you since you were a kid, so eat your food and quit it with the bullshit."

They sat in silence. Ángel picked up his sandwich. It was better not to carry on talking about it. Maybe Daniel was right.

That night, he decided to leave the car on the street and go to the bar. A smell of sweat and beer mingled with dust. The pallid glow of a lamp pierced the clouds of smoke, like a ray of divine light.

Sitting in a corner of the room surrounded by a forest of empty bottles, Lalo and Suazo greeted him with open arms. Dotted between the bottles were plates of corn nuts and yuca fries. Shit, man, you finally showed up!

They had first met a long time ago, and they had run into each other in the street a few times since. Lalo had served with Ángel up in Ayacucho, and it was there that they had met Suazo—Jesus, what a fucked-up time.

The beer tasted increasingly bitter. Every mouthful seemed to make him lighter. Ángel wolfed down a couple of yuca fries. He felt a dry rasp in his throat and started coughing. The conversation carried on. Suazo had just been carjacked by a couple of passengers. Well-dressed men in suits with briefcases had climbed into his taxi, pointed a gun at him, forced him to get out, and then driven off in his car. Suazo had gone to the police to file a report, but he was still shaking with fury. "I'm going to dream about slowly breaking every bone in their bodies. That's what I'll dream about tonight. But I'll tell you something. Let me just tell you something," Suazo said. "D'you want to know what else I dream about? I find myself missing Ayacucho. I wish I was back there. I dream about torturing people, hearing them scream, giving them a few slaps, and then untying them and putting a bullet in them. God, I used to love that. I'd like to . . ."

Suazo did not have time to finish his sentence. In a flash, Ángel was on his feet and had kicked over the table. It boomed like a drum as it hit the floor. The bottles and glasses were shattered. The terracotta tiles were smeared with yuca. Ángel's voice echoed around the bar.

"You miss killing and torturing people, dickwad?

Jesus fuck, you're a piece of shit, man. You're a real piece of shit."

Suazo, who was still sitting down, started to laugh, revealing a row of big, stained teeth.

Ángel grabbed him by the scruff of the neck, hauled him to his feet and punched him in the face. Suazo toppled backward, arms flailing, crashed into a table, and lay motionless.

Seeing him sprawled on the floor, Ángel kicked him several times. Then he lifted him up again and tossed him like a heavy sack. Suazo did not try to defend himself. Lalo grabbed Ángel's arm.

"That's enough, compadre. You'll kill him. Stop it, yeah?"

Ángel released his grip. Blood trickled slowly from Suazo's mouth. He brought a hand up to his face. He was no longer smiling.

"Next time I'll fucking kill you, asshole. You know I will."

A few people at the next table had turned to look. They carried on drinking as they watched. One of them said something: "Fucking lover's quarrel."

Ángel stood there. Lalo was staring at him and Suazo was still sprawled on the floor, legs bent, his arms around his waist. The waiter came over and started to sweep up the shards of glass. What the fuck's wrong with you guys, why do you have to do this shit? You're always smashing things, go on, get the fuck out. Suazo tried to get to his feet, but fell back. Lalo walked over to him and glared at Ángel.

"You do realize that this isn't over?" he said.

The waiter shouted something incomprehensible and walked off. Suazo was still bleeding.

"Nothing is ever over, shitface," Ángel said.

He turned on his heel and left. Outside, the breeze against his face calmed him. He knew that he could not go home.

He started the car. Drove as fast as it would go. The cars he overtook flashed past like bullets fired in the opposite direction.

He pulled up outside Eliana's house.

He checked his watch. Twelve thirty. He felt cold. The lights were out. The flowers shifted in the breeze. The unutterable sadness of the little tree by the window . . .

Ángel lit a cigarette.

He was feeling calmer. It occurred to him that he liked being there, gazing at the window, knowing that she was on the other side (asleep? unable to sleep? watching television?). Ángel drummed his fingers on the steering wheel. She was probably getting on with her life, he thought. Not that he knew exactly what that might mean, but he knew he should leave her in peace. . . . He should not come here so often any more. He should only drop by occasionally. Not talk to her. Not have her see him. Just sit here, be here outside. Gaze at her window, see the glow from her lamp, guess at what she might be doing. And leave a little money for her sometimes. Maybe.

He leaned back, dozed off, woke up thinking it was a new day. It was still dark. He looked at the dashboard clock. A quarter past one.

His hands still ached. Suazo was a tough-skinned bastard.

He lit another cigarette. Took several drags. Later, he would realize that this was what had caught the attention of someone in the house. On the far side of a window, a shadow began to move.

He suddenly saw a figure crossing the dark street.

It was the man who had confronted him before, on this very spot. The man who claimed to be Eliana's father. He was walking toward Ángel.

His baggy trousers flapped. Hand raised. Footsteps pounded on the wet sidewalk.

He slowed as he neared the lamppost. There he was.

"Jesus Christ, not you again," he said. "What are you doing here? What the hell's the matter with you?"

Ángel got out of the car.

"I'm not doing anything. I'm just sitting in my car."

The man gripped his shoulders and started to roar. Ángel could feel the blast of his angry breath on his eyes.

"You've come looking for Eliana, haven't you?"

"That's no business of yours."

The man gave him a shove. Ángel managed to keep his balance. He did not take his eyes from him.

"What do you want with her? Jesus fucking Christ. What the fuck do you want? Tell me why you're looking for her."

"I'm just here, that's all. I want to help her, Señor."

"Go. Get out of here. Go, goddamn it."

The man gave him another shove. Ángel fell, but quickly got to his feet. The sound of the man's voice echoed around the street.

The man was illuminated by the lamppost, though part of his body was still in shadow. He stood, panting, arms hanging by his sides, staring at Ángel.

Then suddenly everything speeded up.

The man had him by the shoulders and was punching and shaking him. Ángel took a step back. He could easily knock this guy out. But he refused to put up a fight. The man was still screaming, pounding a fist into his face and shouting.

Ángel allowed himself to be pushed and punched and managed to stay standing, as though all of this was very remote. Then the man spun him around and threw a punch that shook his bones.

Ángel brought a hand to his face. He clenched his teeth and managed to stay upright. He felt another blow to his cheek. He barely raised his hands. He longed to punch the man as hard as he could. But he did not. "I told you, leave, just leave. Get the fuck out of here. Who are you?"

Ángel leaned against a tree and stared at the man. His body ached. He walked back to the car.

Then something happened. A shadow appeared on the street behind the man.

The slim, slow figure that emerged from the shadows materialized beside them. As the man continued down the road, his fists raised, Ángel saw that it was her.

It was Eliana.

Her slender silhouette, her delicate hands, the hair that fell around her shoulders like a widow's veil. There she was, standing next to him. She raised her arm and held it level.

She was holding something in her hand. A small object. Ángel could just make out the shape of a gun.

As the man continued roaring, she stepped closer and aimed the gun at him. Suddenly, the man who claimed to be her father fell silent. He had seen her approach, had known what was about to happen and he was paralyzed, his eyes boring into her. He said something Ángel did not catch, though it sounded like a plea.

At the last moment, just before he heard the shot, Ángel felt an unexpected breeze and the gentle brush of a hand.

The gunshot was followed by the shriek of startled birds and the sound of wings flapping. Then everything was silent. The man's face became expressionless and he crumpled. From the ground, he stared up at Eliana, his eyes vacant. Blood began to gush from his chest.

Ángel stifled a scream. He turned to his right.

Eliana was holding the gun and calmly looking down at the man she had just killed.

Then she turned to Ángel.

Her eyes blazed with a furious glow. Her body held itself tenuously upright, as though floating. In that moment, she looked like the ghost of a different person, someone Ángel had never seen before. Not a ghost, but a real person from another life. The gun hung loosely from her fingers.

There was a bloody, gaping wound in the man's body, one of his legs was crossed over the other, and his eyes were glassy. Ángel had seen many corpses, but it felt as though this was the first.

Eliana was still standing, watching, as though she was determined to remember this image for the rest of her days.

Ángel took a step back. He wanted to say something but all he could manage were a few curt grunts.

Eliana stepped toward him. For a moment, she stood, staring at him with phosphorescent eyes. She said something that Ángel did not catch. She said it in the same voice with which she had begged him to look for her children.

But, unlike that previous time, Eliana was not lying

on the ground; she was standing in front of him, staring at him. Unlike on that far-off afternoon, it was she who was holding the gun and he who was defenseless. He watched as Eliana raised the gun. She was aiming at him. But in the same movement, she reached out and gently placed the gun in his hand. Ángel felt the brush of her skin as he closed his fingers around the gun she had just given him. It was hard and warm. He raised his head to look at her again.

But she had vanished. The street had engulfed her shadow, there was nothing now but silence and a dark drizzle. He felt as though he had stepped into a tunnel. Somewhere, Ángel saw a door closing.

Everything was suddenly still and silent. Ángel stood alone on the wet asphalt, the whisper of the trees, the bleeding body at his feet, the still-warm pistol in his hand.

The trickle of black blood from the man's body traced a route across the concrete. Around him the silence, like a shapeless monster, engulfed the houses. Ángel looked down at the gun and squeezed it.

In the distance, he heard a dog barking. A bus drove past the intersection.

No one had seen them.

Ángel decided to stay where he was, the wind stinging his eyes, the trail of blood across the sidewalk, the curious angle of the dead man's neck, the shout of a neighbor: what's going on, what's going on, the wail of the approaching siren, a stark, strobing light, the shadowy figures clustering on the sidewalk, the flashing police car surging from the darkness, the cop climbing out and pointing a gun at him. The voice ordering him to get on the ground. The powerful hands of the three cops shoving him into the back of a dirty patrol car.

His face pressed onto the rubber mat on the floor of the car, Ángel did not move as the engine started up. One officer climbed behind the wheel, another held him down, the third was left to stand guard over the body. Put your foot down, compadre, said the officer next to Ángel. We need to get to the station, put in a call to the public prosecutor's office so forensics can come and move the body. No point worrying about the stiff, he's already cold. Let's just get this guy into custody. Can you believe the dumb fuck was still holding the gun? Why did we have to be the ones who got the call, for fuck's sake? I was just coming off shift. Let's get this done and dusted, compadre, and quit it with the whining, we can have some fun later. After we drop this guy off.

III

He could not move his head, the car jolted, wind whistled through the cracked window, lights streaked across the roof of the car. The policeman's boot was pressed against his neck, the sole digging into his cheek and his jaw. The floor of the car juddered, banging his head again and again. But he felt calm.

The officer next to him began to sing something, and from time to time the one glanced around, baring long, gray teeth: life's a bitch, compadre, we caught you red-handed, what did you think would happen. You really are a dumb fuck.

Ángel closed his eyes. Lying on the floor of the police car he felt strangely serene. He felt as though he were flying.

The car screeched to a halt, the officers opened the door, dragged him out and manhandled him up a flight of steps. Ángel found himself in a green building with striped walls, hung with portraits and crucifixes. Everything was a blur of steps, of arms pushing him, and the white haze of fluorescent lights. Then he saw the motto of the Peruvian National Police. "God, Fatherland, Law."

They went into a room. Broken wooden tables, a creased poster ("Our Lady Protects a Noble Officer"), and a computer that cast a blue light onto the wall. An overweight mustachioed officer took his details without looking up. Name, age, offence. Suspected homicide, said one of the officers who had brought him in. Reports of a gunshot. Anonymous call. Attending officers found the suspect still holding the gun. Suspect was standing over the body of the deceased. He was arrested without incident. An ambulance arrived, but as previously stated, the victim was already dead.

The victim was already dead, Ángel said softly. He felt a flicker of joy.

But suddenly he felt very far from what was happening. Watching it as though from a distance. He had done it. He had succeeded.

He spent the night in a holding cell. He lay on the concrete floor, next to him was a puddle of urine, and farther off the huddled shadows of two men. They reeked of sweat and vomit. One had bushy whiskers and was curled up in a corner. The floor was caked with layers of grime. At one point, Ángel pushed himself into a sitting position and leaned against the wall, glancing one way and then the other.

What had happened seemed obvious to him. He should accept the deal she had offered. She was right. And he would be free. He would withdraw from the world for a time. Embrace his fate placidly, happily, almost with love.

After a while he felt tired and lay down again.

In that moment, he was not remotely curious about what was happening to him. It was as though he had deserted his body and would return only once in a while to inspect it. He was in a safe place.

Later he woke with a start in the darkness. The other shadows had melded. The men smelled less pungent than they had some hours earlier.

Ángel recited prayers he had not said in years. He was not seeking consolation, he simply wanted to prove to himself that he was really here, that he had not lost his memory. Then he reached into his pocket and took out the two photographs he always kept with him and began to talk to them. I'm here, Mamá. Don't worry.

He fell asleep again. When he woke, dawn had broken. Someone was banging on the bars.

An officer accompanied him to a public phone next to the captain's office. He had some small change and called his brother Daniel.

"I'm in jail."

There was a long silence on the other end.

"What's going on?"

"Someone died."

"Died? Who died?"

"Some guy. I'm at the police station."

Another silence.

Ángel bit his lip. He could picture Daniel glancing at the clock, muttering something under his breath, reassuring Marissa.

"I'll be there as soon as I can," he said at length.

Ángel hung up.

"Come with me," said the officer.

From that point, everything seemed to happen very quickly.

He followed the officer to a room. Sitting at a plastic table, an officer with stripes on his uniform was waiting for him in front of a computer. We have the incident report, the officer told him, but we need your version of events. To get a complete picture.

Ángel offered a few comments. The guy had threatened him. There had been a struggle. The man's gun had gone off, he had picked it up. That was all.

He was taken back to the cell. He sat in a corner. He

heard a voice. Someone nearby was talking to him, but Ángel could barely hear.

Half an hour later, his brother, Daniel, showed up.

He had brought two pieces of bread, some ham, and a plastic beaker of black coffee. Why did you kill this guy? Did you actually kill him? Who was he? I never imagined you'd end up in this situation. I don't know what you're going to do. Has this got something to do with the woman you've been looking for?

Ángel did not answer.

They say they found you with a gun in your hand, standing next to a body, it's what they call *in flagrante delicto*, Daniel said. Out there the public prosecutor is meeting with the officer who interviewed you. They're talking. We need to get you a defense attorney as soon as possible. They're going to send the report to the public prosecutor's office. The investigating magistrate will decide whether you're guilty, then the National Penitentiary Institute will decide which prison to send you to. Because from what I can tell, there's no way of avoiding a prison sentence, *hermanito*. What would Mamá say if she could see you now?

Ángel looked at his brother. Sweat trickled down his cheek. Daniel kept his hands clasped in front of him as he spoke, as though trying to distance himself from the situation. Did you really kill this guy? I can't believe it.

Ángel nodded.

"I think I'd had a lot to drink. I met up with Lalo and Suazo and I was knocking them back. And then on the street, some guy showed up and threatened me. I don't know what came over me."

"But who was he?"

"I don't know. Some guy who showed up, threatening

me and shoving me around. I'd been drinking with Lalo and Suazo. I don't know. I can't really remember."

"But what the fuck were you doing there? It's not exactly on your way home."

Daniel looked at him as he shook his head.

"I don't know. I don't remember."

His eyes met those of his brother. He could see a mixture of rebuke and pity.

"Okay, listen," Daniel said. "I'll be back this afternoon with something to eat. We have to arrange it so they send you to San Jorge. The other prisons are horrendous. Problem is, San Jorge is reserved for first-time offenders, but defendants on a murder charge aren't usually sent there. Then again, your case isn't straightforward. I honestly don't believe you killed this guy. And even if you did, it wasn't premeditated. Right. I'm going to need to pull a few strings, I'll see what I can do."

One of the shadows in the corner of the cell suddenly gave a roar that sounded like a roar of laughter.

"Who decides?"

"The National Penitentiary Institute decides which prison you're sent to. We'll see how it goes. But you need to be in San Jorge. It's your best option, considering the circumstances."

"Thanks, Daniel. And I'm sorry about all this. I don't know what else to say."

Ángel found himself alone again. All he could see was the image of Eliana handing him the gun, the bloodstains on the body, the flashing lights and the wail of the sirens, the officers hauling him away.

In the afternoon, Daniel returned with a bag of bread rolls, some ham, and a bottle of juice. Ángel was not very hungry, but he knew that his body was weak and he needed to eat something.

A couple of days later, Ángel was transferred to San Jorge prison.

Daniel had called in a favor from a friend in the judiciary. San Jorge was the best possible result, under the circumstances. A few years later, such a thing would have been impossible, Ángel would realize in hindsight, but at the time it was still feasible.

When he heard the iron gate clang behind him, he was convinced that he would never leave.

The prison was a low, squat building on La Colmena, with walls of pale blue bricks surmounted by a tall wire fence punctuated by black watchtowers. A wide sidewalk planted with palm trees separated it from the two-lane avenue. A large iron gate with two barred windows stood in front, around which hawkers clustered, selling chocolate, candy, and newspapers.

The iron gate opened and closed quickly to allow guards in and out.

Inside, the prison was a series of corridors, courtyards, and low cell blocks.

Ángel spent his first night sleeping in the First Offenders' Block. He could just make out the courtyard, the concrete annex, and the line of the other buildings and, beyond, the vast expanse of time without daylight. He felt overwhelmed by the weight of reality bearing down on him, and prayed to his mother and to the Virgen de las Nieves for the strength he would need to be alone with himself.

On the second day, Ángel was moved to a cell with

four bunks. He would have to share the toilet in the corner with his three cellmates. Each man had hung a small curtain around his bed to separate himself from the others and create a small area of privacy. On the walls, his cellmates had hung calendars, pictures of women, prayers, and family photos. At night, some would listen to music on battery-powered radios. The first night, Ángel was kept awake by the snoring of the other men. He would have to get used to it.

In the days that followed, he felt as though he had taken over the body of another man. He became accustomed to this new identity, sheltered by the whistling sound that came from the walls. A sound that could transform itself into a bullet and ricochet around the cell, banging off the walls and the curtains hung around the bunks.

In those early days, Ángel heard other sounds too, sounds he had never imagined. Some prisoners would laugh or sob. Others would stare silently at the ceiling. One stroked a doll, his eyes vacant. Ángel found the stench unbearable, though it was occasionally alleviated by a breeze.

Each block had its own canteen with red plastic tables and chairs. The menu included beans, *shambar* soup, and pork and potato stew. But there were also stalls selling *lomo saltado* and *ají de gallina*. Most of the prisoners had food brought in by their families.

In the morning, over breakfast in the canteen, Ángel would chat with the other inmates. Sometimes they would ask what he was in for. What brings you here, what happened? one of them laughed. He usually avoided answering, but sometimes he would tell them he had been charged with murdering a man. Murdering someone is always a good idea, one man said with a smile. I wish I'd murdered some guy, but I'm in here for fraud.

A day came when Ángel was able to look at himself in a mirror. He realized that he had a new face. The lines were sharper, his eyes looked smaller and harder. A sort of calm held his lips in place. He felt as though it had been a long time since he had last looked at himself.

The routine every day was more or less the same. Cells were unlocked at 6 a.m. Ángel would go for a walk or jog with other prisoners around the large courtyard. Breakfast was served at 7 a.m., usually bread, porridge, sometimes luncheon meat. Roll call was at 8 a.m. After that, inmates were free to attend workshops: cabinet-making, tailoring, carpentry, ceramics, shoemaking. One morning a warden came and asked which workshops he wanted to sign up for.

"Ceramics and shoemaking," Ángel said. "Let's see what I can do."

On his first Sunday there, Daniel came to visit. They sat at one of the tables in the courtyard and talked.

"How have you been feeling?"

Ángel shrugged.

"I'm here until further notice. They've said I can join a workshop. I've signed up for ceramics and shoemaking."

"I can provide you with potter's clay and leather, if you like," Daniel said. "I can get you barbotine too. They've told me that's what they use here. I can bring some in this evening."

The following day, Ángel walked into a large hall furnished with a few workbenches. This was the cobbler's workshop. There was a clicker press to cut the leather, a stitching machine, and an air compressor.

From time to time, guards would wander into the

workshops. Occasionally, a cat sauntered past. It had gotten into the prison from one of the neighboring rooftops and, to judge by its gaze, felt perfectly happy on the inside.

Ángel decided he would make shoes that he could sell during Wednesday and Sunday visits. A week later, Daniel brought him more of the leather. He also brought potter's clay and barbotine—something Ángel had never heard of, but he discovered it was simply clay dissolved in water. He would pay Daniel back as soon as he could.

In time, Ángel adjusted to the routine. Every morning, after breakfast, he would either go to the ceramics or the leather workshop, organize his materials, and set to work. He enjoyed turning a few strips of leather and shoelaces into a pair of polished shoes. He found the work engrossing. When he first laid eyes on a pair of patent leather shoes, he felt as though he were looking at some recently uncovered treasure.

By noon, he usually felt exhausted but happy with the progress he had made on the leather uppers and the soles. After lunch, he would rest for a while, and in the afternoon, he would go back to the workshop. On Wednesdays and Saturdays he offered the shoes for sale. On Sundays he gave the money to his brother to buy more leather.

Some nights he had time to read. Daniel had brought in some books, a few novels and *Biographies of Great Men*. The other prisoners found the idea of reading in there strange, though occasionally someone would ask to borrow a novel. He also borrowed books from the prison's Ricardo Palma library.

After a considerable time, he began to attend Mass on Thursdays and Sundays. He did not follow the ceremony, but he would sit, listen to the priest, and meditate. It was an opportunity to try and understand how the readings and the sermons were connected to what was going on. He was moved by the story of Job, a man who lost everything yet still believed in God.

One day a new priest named Esteban arrived, an affable man with a wide, dimpled face and long, jaunty eyebrows. Father Esteban was talkative and invariably had something to say on any topic, from the weather to current affairs. He talked about religion only when somebody asked him a question.

"I'm not sure, but I feel as though I know you from somewhere," Esteban said when they first met.

Over time, Father Esteban's visits became more and more frequent. He would show up on Saturdays to play five-a-side soccer and would sometimes help out in the workshops. On Thursdays and Sundays, he celebrated Mass. His sermons always seemed to sum up the feelings of the prisoners. Father Esteban told stories from the Bible and made connections with what the men were going through. Ángel considered telling him one day what had happened.

One Sunday, Don Paco came to visit.

"You never told me you were bored working in the store," he said, laughing. "You were so desperate to go to prison you had to kill a guy."

"Sorry for abandoning you, Paco."

"Don't worry. I'm quitting the job too, actually. I'm packing up and going home, Angelito. To be honest, selling things isn't for me. At my age, I've already sold off my time and my life, so I'd rather buy any old thing from the market to make up for it, excuse the bad joke."

They talked for a long time that day. Don Paco was

one of the few people he would miss from the outside world.

One day, as he was leaving the workshop, a young man came up to him and introduced himself as his lawyer. He was thin, with a good-natured smile and the small, pointed head of an old tortoise. He moved slowly, and always looked at things sidelong and from below. His name was Hugo Longo.

"Pleased to meet you," the lawyer said, proffering his hand.

Ángel sat with him at a table with three chairs in a corridor whose walls were plastered with inspirational quotations ("You are the architect of your own destiny"). Longo took out a pen and a notebook.

He considered Ángel with his large, gentle eyes and then gave a short speech about his case:

"There are a number of factors in our favor. First, although neighbors saw you arguing with the victim on the street, no one actually saw you shoot him. Besides, their statements to the police were conflicting and contradictory. At first, they said they saw the victim struggling with a man, and then they said something completely different. In addition, the victim was notorious in the neighborhood for stirring up trouble. Señor Huarón—the deceased—routinely harassed passersby, he would storm out of his house yelling and screaming. Several people had filed complaints against him. Finally, on the night of your arrest, the police did not carry out tests for gunshot residue on you; this was a grave error on the part of the arresting officers and the superintendent, it was negligent. They were so convinced of your guilt that they charged you without carrying out the test. But you might have been confused. The fact that you were standing nearby holding the gun could be considered circumstantial. This was ample, credible, up-to-date evidence, irrefutable evidence of your innocence. You did not kill him. You found yourself standing there with the gun. Did you know the deceased? (I don't know, Ángel said.) Why then did you confess? Someone had made an anonymous call to the police from a public phone, a fact that seemed very strange. Who had made the call? The real murderer?

"In your initial statement, Señor Ángel, you claimed that you killed him because he had threatened you. Killed him without premeditation or malicious intent, in self-defense. It was a moment of confusion. Did you bring the gun?"

"No. It was the victim's gun. He threatened me, I wrestled the gun off him and, in the struggle, I shot him. That's what happened."

"Okay, very good," said Longo. "But some neighbors claim they saw you arguing with this man on a previous occasion. They say they saw him shoving and harassing you that night. But there's a problem. As it turns out, the dead man had numerous enemies. And you could have been sent by one of them to kill him. According to the arresting officers, your breath smelled strongly of alcohol that night, which is not a good thing, obviously, but it's something we can overcome. A man can be a drunk without being a murderer, Señor. They're not the same thing at all."

Longo was quiet. He seemed satisfied with what he had said.

"Who was the dead man?" asked Ángel. "Tell me."

Longo touched his chin.

"The deceased was Señor Oswaldo Huarón, a local resident."

"What do you know about him?"

"He was originally from Ayacucho, he lived there during the war, and he had previously been arrested for violent and drunken behavior. He lived on Calle Alipio Ponce."

"I didn't know him."

"That's exactly what we need you to say in your testimony," said Longo. "True, some neighbors had previously heard you arguing, but as I said before—sorry for repeating myself—no one saw you shoot him. There's no way around it. Moreover, there's no history of any quarrel between you. Second, there's the matter of the gunshot residue test. Third, the gun was not registered to you. . . . It was an army-issue revolver that had been declared lost, there was no registered owner. You have to say that you didn't do it. You know how easily influenced judges are."

"But I already said I did it. It was an accident."

"You need to retract your statement. This is perfectly possible—sorry for repeating myself. There are legal provisions. You saw a man running away."

"But I killed him," said Ángel.

"No, you didn't. That's why I'm here, to prove that you didn't. I'm your defense attorney. You did not kill him, Señor Ángel. I believe you found the gun lying next to the body and picked it up. And then you forgot what had happened. Amnesia. This is a case of amnesia, you're a little absent-minded, a lot of people are, I know plenty. But that's no problem. You saw a man running from the scene of the crime. Someone else killed this man. That's how I see it. That's what happened, Señor Serpa."

Ángel sat in silence.

"Well, maybe . . . ," he said after a moment. "I think I picked up the gun and I was holding it when the officers showed up. The truth is, I did see a man running away."

Longo's eyes lit up.

"Why didn't you say this in your statement to the police?"

Ángel shrugged.

"The truth is, I don't know whether or not I killed him. You're right. I think I saw a man running away."

Longo scratched his chin with his long, gray nails.

"Let's see what we can do, then."

"I may have seen someone running away, I'm not sure. The thing is, I don't want someone else to be charged."

"That would be the ideal outcome. To find out who really did it. But let's see."

"Look, do whatever you want. Who's paying you?"

The attorney put away his notepad.

"Your brother Daniel is paying my fees and expenses."

From outside came the sound of people playing soccer. Some of the inmates were in the crafts workshop. Others were strolling around the yard with their hands in their pockets. This is what Ángel would have been doing had he not been meeting with the attorney.

"I'm here to help you," Longo said. "For me it is a fundamental part of serving my fellow humans, including you." Longo stared at him. "But there not much I can do if you don't do your part," he added.

"I'm here," said Ángel.

"But your mind seems to be elsewhere."

Longo raised his eyebrows, got to his feet and headed toward the door.

"Well, anyway . . ."

"Señor Longo."

The attorney turned around.

"Can you tell me more about him?"

"I'm sorry?"

"About the man who died. Señor Huarón, I think you said his name was?"

"He lived locally."

"What else do we know about him?"

"People say he was a bastard. A lecher. Apparently, he was always trying it on with girls in the barrio. He was originally from Ayacucho, everyone knew him because he told stories about the war. He was a loudmouth, people say. And, with women, he couldn't keep his hands to himself. That's the kind of guy he was. That's why his neighbors think what you did was score-settling, that's what they say. That you're probably the brother of one of his victims. But, as we know, you had no connection to any of them. So that theory is a non-starter."

The attorney trailed off.

"And this Señor Huarón, what was he doing there that night?" Ángel asked.

"He lived there. On that street. He lived nearby. What were you doing there?"

"I make deliveries—crockery, glasses, home furnishings. I was working at a store. I had stopped for a rest—you know how it is. I fell asleep. Do you genuinely believe I didn't kill him, Señor Longo?"

"Of course you didn't. And I'm going to get you out of here."

Longo nodded by way of goodbye and left.

Ángel looked out the window. If the dead man's name was Huarón, he could not have been Eliana's father. Her surname was Cauti. He was probably some local loudmouth who had been harassing her, a bastard, a son-of-a-bitch, probably, boasting that he was her father. So, in freeing her from him, he had done something good.

Ángel felt a breeze. Out in the yard, the game of five-a-side soccer carried on. He heard a shout. Somebody had scored. He should go outside and celebrate with them.

After the first few weeks, he began to get used to life in prison. The days mounted up. In the morning, after exercise and breakfast, he would alternate between the shoe-making and ceramics workshops.

Over time, Ángel became more interested in ceramics and spent less time making shoes. He used barbotine to create figurines of dogs, of lovers next to the Eiffel Tower, of bulls about to charge. After he had finished, he glazed them and put them on display for the buyers and brokers to see.

One day he met Sinesio, who was on remand for the attempted murder of his wife. Sinesio had told the story over and over. He had surprised his wife in a hotel room with her lover and, without a second thought, had shot them both. He had not actually killed them, but it had been close. They had reported him to the police and gone to live elsewhere. Sinesio had no regrets. No way. "Obviously, I'm still in love with her, I have no problem admitting it, but that's just the way it goes sometimes, as my late father would say. At least I scared the fuckers shitless."

Sinesio was heavyset, taciturn, and had large jowls. He could spend hours adding filigree work to the leather objects he made. Once, he had made a saddle and put it up for sale. Somewhere out there, Sinesio would say excitedly, a beautiful woman is riding a horse with my saddle. I can almost feel her, if you can believe that.

Sinesio was still waiting for his trial, though he claimed he did not care about getting out. He could not bear to be out in the world without his wife, even if she was a fucking cheat. She now lived far away, with that disgusting insect of a lover. But don't go thinking I regret what I did, he would insist. I gave them a good scare. I bet they still see me every night. See me standing by the bed with my gun, I reckon. And I bet when he sees me, he can't get it up. That would be good.

Sinesio soon moved to the ceramics workshop and began working alongside Ángel.

Dimas Donayre also turned up, an ex-soccer player in prison on fraud charges. He had spent years embezzling money from his company. He had not done it out of need, but simply because he enjoyed stealing money from the owners, who had never treated him well. Dimas was tall and angular, with sharp features. He had the keen eyes of a falcon, flickering from side to side, constantly looking for something. It was a tic from his years as the goal-keeper with a second-division team.

At lunch, Ángel would stand in line with Dimas and Sinesio, and they would sit together to eat. They spoke little, between long pauses. One of their favorite dishes was *olluco* with rice, one of the few delicacies on the canteen menu.

One of the guards, a man named Ocharán, made a living trying to extort money from prisoners, offering to buy them food from outside. If he noticed a prisoner who seemed nervous, he took advantage, sometimes using threats and beatings. Ángel knew he needed to keep his head down and try to ignore him. There was something vaguely corrupt about the way Ocharán looked. He had curly hair and a broad smile, and he strolled around with his hand out, as though forever looking for someone to extort or threaten. He had tried approaching Ángel on a number of occasions, but Ángel barely acknowledged him.

Daniel usually visited on Sundays. Don Paco also came to see him. He told Ángel that the store owner had quickly replaced him with a young man called Luchito who occasionally stole glasses. But I'm too old to be a snitch, he added.

Sometimes on Wednesdays, which were reserved for female visitors, his sister-in-law, Marissa, would come. "I don't believe it," said Tania, who also came to visit a couple of times. "You're not that kind of man. I can't imagine you killing anyone." Her stall on Surquillo market was increasingly popular. "But I miss you, Señor Ángel," she said. "It's such a shame you made a mistake."

His attorney continued to visit, offering nuggets of hope that Ángel took for facts. Zambo Samson and El Gordo John also came by. "Don't tell me you actually whacked that fucker, I don't believe a fucking word," El Gordo said.

The fights were not going well, El Gordo told him. Every night there are fewer monsters, he explained. There's a lot more construction work around these days, and the monsters find jobs hauling bricks. Some are now reformed characters, for fuck's sake. It's a disaster.

Having started out counting the days and the weeks he had been there, Ángel soon lost track of the time he had spent in the cell, the workshops, and the exercise yard. But one day Ángel realized that he had been there for exactly ten months. Longo had not been able to get him released, but he had managed to have the trial brought forward, an exceptional feat according to the other inmates.

Renzo, the man who slept in the bunk opposite, had his wall plastered with photos of women in bikinis. They're my friends, he would say in a husky voice. They sleep here with me. Ángel would have liked to put some photos of Eliana on his wall.

Over the months, he had thought about her often. He wondered whether she still lived on Calle Alipio Ponce, what had happened after the man died, whether she was worried that he might tell the truth about what had happened that night. Did she include him in her prayers when she went to church? It cheered him to think that he had been in her thoughts during this time. He wondered whether she had told anyone what had really happened. He had never felt tempted to admit that *she* had murdered the man who claimed to be her father, then handed him the gun.

When the day came for his trail at the Palacio de Justicia, he felt nervous. He would be in a room with judges, a prosecutor, and an audience. Everyone would be staring at him.

That morning Ángel put on a three-piece suit his brother had brought him. The tie was blue, the jacket gray, his face ashen with fear. He noticed he had a few more gray hairs, which made him look respectable. "You need to look innocent," Daniel said. "Don't forget, appearances are important. It's not just who you are, it's how you come across. We need to make sure you scrub up well, because right now you look like a crazy man."

Ángel arrived at the Palacio de Justicia prepared to try and forget where he was. The preliminary hearing was to take place in the Superior Court of Lima. He walked into the courtroom and took a seat at the table next to Longo, after one of the guards showed him where the defendant sits. He was not far from the judges' bench where three magistrates were seated, looking through documents and talking in low voices. On the far side of the room was the prosecutor.

The three magistrates wore sashes adorned with gold medals and the flag of Peru. Behind them was a red curtain, and the flags of Peru and of the judiciary. There was a crucifix on the bench.

It pained him to see his brother and sister-in-law sitting in the public gallery. He did not want to put them through this ordeal. Simply being here was horribly shameful. But there was no alternative.

There were three or four other people in the gallery whom Ángel, fortunately, did not know. He assumed they were simply gawkers who found it entertaining to see somebody being tried for something. They were simply waiting for the sentence to be handed down.

It was time to begin. The prosecutor did not take his eyes off Ángel.

He was not sure whether to take Longo's advice and change his testimony. There had been no struggle. I found the gun on the ground and picked it up. Would anyone believe him? He decided that he *had* seen a man running away from the scene.

Longo began his opening statement. His strident voice was a result of his "overwhelming" emotion. He was like a tribune of the people, facing the great court. His ear-splitting tone was accompanied by sweeping gesticulations, as though the court were an apathetic orchestra that he was doing his best to conduct.

Longo's voice filled the space. My esteemed client admitted to killing the man, but at a time when he was in a highly confused state. To expand on the evidence, I draw your attention to the fact that no paraffin test for gunshot residue was carried out on my client, hence there is no conclusive forensic evidence, or, to put it simply, no conclusive evidence. Furthermore, there are witness statements alleging that someone else was at the scene of the crime.

After a pause he added: Even the neighbors who made these statements cannot identify the person who committed the crime, since the real culprit fled the scene.

The judges studied Ángel. One of them, a man with a protruding jaw, bushy eyebrows, and beady eyes, gave him an amused smile. He seemed to be thinking about what he would do when this was over. He might even be prepared to believe Ángel was innocent, if it meant getting out sooner.

All through the proceedings, Ángel watched Daniel's face. His brother was seated in the front row. Ángel felt moved by his enduring generosity: his financial support, his regular visits, his pulling strings in the justice system. He felt indebted, although that was not quite right. Daniel's generosity made him feel ashamed, but it also inspired him, and, in a way, gave him a reason to carry on. His brother was here, in court, his face a mask of concern, when he could just as easily have been in his office or with his family. Ángel had to respond to his presence in some way.

The attorney carried on speaking. Ángel felt that he should react. What should he say? In that moment, he had no memory of Longo's instructions. He had never expected to have to say anything, but merely to sit and watch.

When his turn came to testify, he paid attention to his every word. Longo was right. He had found Señor Huarón dead. He had picked up the gun after he had seen the body. No, he didn't know why he had picked it up, maybe out of curiosity. Yes, out of curiosity. He was innocent. He had seen a man running away. A thickset man in white shirt, sneakers, and black trousers. He had seen the man only for a second, obviously. He would not be able to identify him.

The prosecutor was in his seat.

"But this is not what you said when you were arrested. You said there had been an altercation."

"I must have been confused."

"Confused?"

"Yes. The truth is, I found him dead. I saw a man running away and I picked up the gun."

"No one in this court believes a word you say," said the prosecutor. "Not one word."

The prosecutor had a round face, the eyes of a toad and a bald spot half-covered by a comb-over. He wore a shiny black three-piece suit. He sat in his seat, almost completely still. His eyes had the fastidious cruelty of the disaffected. Ángel imagined that he had spent years trying to become a judge without success. This was the reason he was the way he was.

He turned back to listen to his attorney. Longo punched the air and in a deep, authoritative voice explained that a neighbor had heard a shot and, a moment later, had peered out the window and seen his client at the scene of the crime, holding the gun. That is the evidence, your honors. He clarified: That is the evidence that led to the wrong man being charged. The witness did not see my client commit the crime; she saw him standing there only *after* the man had died. And the witness in question has disappeared, I might add.

Longo opened his briefcase and took out a piece of paper. I have the evidence here, he said. Then he passed the neighbor's sworn statement to the magistrates. According to the statement, there had been an altercation before the gunshot rang out. That much was true. But no one had been able to track down this witness since. Where was she?

"Let him say what he likes," Ángel muttered to himself.

"From this, we can conclude that nobody saw him fire the gun," Longo added. "This charge has no basis in law or in fact. I beseech you. My reasoning is very clear."

The magistrates were staring at him.

The prosecutor approached Ángel.

"Did you or did you not know the deceased, Señor Oswaldo Huarón?" he asked.

Ángel said nothing.

"Answer the question."

"Yes, I'd seen him in that neighborhood."

The prosecutor stood next to him. His eyes were hard as splinters of glass.

"Tell us again your version of what happened on the night of the incident in question. Let's see what you can tell us, Señor Serpa."

Ángel replied that on the night in question he had been driving around the neighborhood, he had just dropped off a delivery from the store and had stopped to take a rest. He had dozed off without realizing. When he woke up, he saw the man walking toward him. Huarón had begun threatening him for no reason. He had been carrying a gun. Then a thickset man had appeared, wrested the gun from him, and shot him. Ángel had picked it up only as the police arrived. The killer had run off.

"And what were you doing in the neighborhood that day?"

Ángel replied:

"I've just told you. I was working in a store. I'd just made a delivery. I felt tired and I fell asleep in the car. When I woke up, it was dark. It was late. And then I saw someone shoot the man. He was a fat guy, it was very dark, he fled the scene. I didn't get a good look at him."

"But neighbors say they had seen you in the area previously."

"A delivery man gets around, Señor."

"Yes, I know. I know. Now, you say that Señor Huarón was threatening you?"

Ángel realized that everything that he was saying was true. He felt as though he were reconstructing the scene in his mind, as he imagined it and as he was describing it.

The prosecutor spoke in a slow, shrill voice. His words were barely audible, but there was a muted rage in the sounds he was making. He stared at Ángel with his fish eyes.

A silence had fallen over the courtroom, punctured by the coughing of Daniel and Marissa. Next to them sat El Gordo.

"Yes, he was threatening me. I'd been in the area before and he had threatened me then, too."

"Do you know why the man was threatening you?"

Ángel hesitated before answering.

"No, I don't know. I think he was a bit cracked, but I don't know."

"So, why had you been in the neighborhood previously?"

Ángel pursed his lips together. Considered what he was about to say. The most important thing was not to mention Eliana's name.

"Like I told you. I make deliveries. . . . We have a lot of customers in the neighborhood. . . . I don't remember their names, but I'd been in the area before. . . . And I don't know why he had threatened me before. . . . I didn't know the guy."

"It is important to take into account that Señor Huarón had many enemies," Longo said, "any of whom might have been in the area, committed the murder, and fled the scene. This is the most likely explanation. We know all about Señor Huarón's activities, he was a man of dubious moral character, there's no need to say more."

The statements and testimonies had come to an end. The principal magistrate brought the session to a close. The verdict would be given in two days.

That night, as he stepped into his cell, Ángel felt relief.

"I think it's going to be tough call," Longo had said when they parted company.

Longo was right.

On the day of the verdict, the judge cited a number of reasons why they had found Señor Ángel Serpa guilty of the murder of Señor Oswaldo Huarón, albeit with no aggravating circumstances. The sentence was fifteen years.

That following Sunday, Longo came to visit him.

"We could have done something, but you wouldn't play ball."

"No. I'm sorry."

"I need to win this case. I'm planning to appeal."

"Do what you like. I'll be here."

The next morning, Ángel transferred to the art workshop. He had an image of what he wanted to paint, but no sooner did his paintbrush touch the Bristol board than his hand went in another direction. There were cactuses, the sun, green hills. There was not a single human being.

The following Sunday, at around eleven, his brother Daniel showed up. He smiled a brief, cheerless smile.

"I just worked out what really happened," he said. "It's obvious—that woman you told me about . . . she killed him. Right? Be honest with me."

"What makes you think that?"

Daniel grabbed him by the arm.

"I don't know why it didn't occur to me sooner. She did it. But you're trying to protect this woman. You had nothing to do with the murder, but you're covering for her. This is the same woman you told me about, the one you wanted to give money to. She killed him, didn't she?"

"I don't know."

"Well, I know. From what I've been able to find out, this guy Huarón had rescued the woman called Eliana. He'd met her up in Ayacucho during the war and even lived with her for a while. But I'm going to do some more digging."

"Who told you all this?"

"I got it from of the neighbors last night."

"Who told you to go looking for people in the neighborhood?"

"Your friend, Cholo Palacios. He cleared up a few other things."

"What did he say?"

"He told me you'd been looking for information in the registry office."

"He shouldn't have told you that."

Daniel's face slowly began to light up. Suddenly he got up and stood beside the table.

"So, I figure what happened is she killed the guy and now you're taking the blame. She left you to pass yourself off as the murderer so she would be free. It's blatantly obvious. You did it to atone to her. Am I right? Tell the truth, Mamá can hear you."

His eyes were swollen and he was breathing heavily.

"It wasn't like that, but it doesn't matter."

"What do you mean it doesn't matter?"

Ángel shrugged.

"I killed him. And I'm happy with this."

"What?"

"I like being in here."

"I don't understand, *hermanito*."

"In here I don't have to worry about getting up early to go work in a store, about some guy breaking my jaw in a fight. In here, I feel safe. I feel calm. I don't have to think about anything except my figurines and my shoes and my paintings. I like it. And I have friends."

"What friends?"

"I've got lots of friends: Sinesio, Dimas, Father Esteban. I hang out with them."

Daniel rubbed his face. In that moment, Ángel felt as though his brother was a complete stranger.

"You need to get out of here, compadre. What will Mamá think up in heaven?"

"She already knows."

"Knows what?"

"I tell her everything. Besides, I don't see the point of getting out. I'll get out some day. It's not like I'll be here my whole life."

"I told Mamá I'd look after you. The day she died, I held her hand and I told her I'd look out for you. In her last moments, she was worried about you."

"Yes, I know. But Mamá is looking down on us now and I know she thinks I'm right."

They sat for a moment in silence.

There was a distant roar of traffic from the avenue: a rumble of engines punctuated by the sound of car horns, overlapping voices, the occasional shout. Ángel had become accustomed to these sounds, but just then, they seemed new.

"I don't know how I ended up with an idiot like you for a brother," Daniel said. "I honestly don't get it."

Ángel smiled.

"That's just the way it is, I'm afraid."

Daniel looked at him, his eyes wide.

"So, tell me. Who do you talk to in here?"

Ángel took out the photographs. The faces of his mother and the captain.

"Like I told you before, I talk to them."

"These are your friends."

"I've always got something to tell them."

"Right, it's obvious now that you're crazy, compadre. I'm leaving."

Seeing Daniel get to his feet, Ángel felt a sharp twinge in his chest. He stood up and faced him. He did not want his brother to leave.

"Daniel."

"What?"

"I want to thank you, Daniel," he said, raising a hand. "I don't know what I would have done without you. Long before I ended up here, I don't know what I would have done. If it wasn't for you, I'd be dead. I don't know where

I'd be. And not just because you've helped me out. But because I feel like at least one person gives a damn about me. I don't know how to thank you, *hermano*. I mean it. It's true."

Daniel clapped his hands over his eyes. Then he looked at his brother.

"That's all very well, but you're not doing anything to help yourself."

"I'm sorry. I don't know what's wrong with me, that's the truth."

Daniel held his hands up.

"I don't know what's wrong with you either, Angelito. I don't know why you feel so guilty. It's like you don't want to live, for fuck's sake."

Ángel suddenly felt a profound sense of calm wash over him. Out in the yard, a group of men in overalls walked past with brooms and buckets.

"I do want to live, I just don't want to live the way I have been up to now."

"Well, let's see what we can do to get you out of here. That's the most important thing. You didn't murder anyone."

Daniel went to the gate and called the guard.

"How can you be so sure that I didn't murder him?"

"Sorry, but you're not capable of killing anybody."

Daniel called the guard again.

"You're wrong, *hermano*. I did kill him. I knew he was a bastard. I killed him so they'd put me in prison."

"But why?"

"Because I was tired . . ."

"Tired of what?"

"Of what? Of getting up every morning, going to the store, making deliveries, having to worry about the brakes and the oil for the station wagon, of waking up alone and of talking to the bedroom walls, to the photo of Mamá and the other photo. Of spending my nights wrestling, waking up with bruises, of spending time with asshole *luchadores*. All that shit really fucked my head up. And now it doesn't. Nothing gets to me now. I can read, I can work, I can make my figurines. I bunk up with three other guys, but I don't care. If some night I feel like I'm going to die, I can talk to them about whatever pops into my mind. Like a memory of when we were kids and life was good, remember? There was a time when life was good. Sometimes, it's all I can think about. It was such a long time ago."

Daniel smiled.

"That's in the past, Ángel. The important thing is for life to be good in the present. The present is what matters," he said, pointing to the ground.

"Life is good again now," said Ángel. "I have a few friends. I'm going to start painting. I'd like to make churches someday. I recently figured out the right mixture. Do you want me to tell you? I fire the clay in the kiln, let it cool, and then paint it. I know how now. Then I'll sell them and I'll make a little money. It's thanks to you that I'm able to do this, I know. I'm grateful. I owe you. But the thing that saves me, that truly saves me is knowing that I made this. That I can do this."

Daniel sat down next to him. He scratched his head.

"Well, that's something I do understand."

Ángel looked at him. His brother sat with his head tilted back, just as he used to sit at the dining table when they were children.

"That's the thing, Daniel. Making something. That's what I want. To make things. My own things. Get up in the morning and tell myself I'm going to make something that's mine, then make it. This is all new to me and it makes me happy. Makes me feel like someone else. There's nothing like finding out that you can make something that's yours and no one else's, that no one else could have made the sculpture—a bull, a horse, a dog—that you made. I am completely in the present, or I'm beyond time, that's where I want to be, beyond time, I don't think about what's going to happen, I don't think about getting out of here, and I don't think about what I did during the war or any of that shit. And it was shit, but sometimes I realize I can't go on thinking about the war. I don't think about anything. I'm aware that I'm here, nothing more. Just that. I know I'm here making something that no one else has made—it doesn't matter what, any old thing. And believe it or not, that's all I need. I make my figurines. My ceramic figures. And then I look at them and I know that I've made something only I could have made. And I think about that. And sometimes, when I'm alone I pray. I pray from time to time, in case you're interested. But I pray to myself sometimes too, when I dare, and pray to God, although God isn't the problem. There's no problem. It's just me and my things, and knowing that I've got you, that's all."

Daniel was staring at his brother. A smile crept over his face.

"And what are you going to do with yourself afterward?"

"Afterward? I've no idea."

"Listen, Angelito. I don't think you're as happy in here as you say. You need to think about what's going to happen afterward."

"I don't think about that."

Daniel held up his hands, as though in surrender.

"Maybe I'll just leave you to it, then. Come back and see you in a couple of years."

"No, no. Don't leave me, Daniel. Please."

Ángel could barely speak. His voice came in faltering bursts.

"You're all I've got. That's the truth. The only thing. You, Marissa, and your kids."

They looked at one another. In the corridor, someone screamed.

"Okay, let's talk about something else. Some bad news just for a change. The building you used to live in was flooded. The pipes burst and water started streaming out. It's been declared uninhabitable."

"Well, what can you do? What about my car?"

"I had to sell it to pay the attorney. There was no problem since it was in my name."

"Well, that's good."

Daniel leaned closer.

"Listen, Ángel. When you get out of here, I don't want you going back to being a salesman. Not anymore."

"No. Not anymore. I'll see what I'll do. But I'm not much good at anything, you know. You were always the one who knew how to do things. I was always pretty useless. That's why I thought joining the army would help. But it didn't. It made things worse."

"You know why you joined up."

Ángel looked at him.

"Yes, I know."

"As for the rest, we'll see whether or not you're useless."

The guard popped his head around the door. The two brothers were standing close together. Daniel held out his hand, but Ángel hugged him.

"It's one o'clock. Lunchtime. You can come back this afternoon, if you like," the guard said.

Daniel nodded.

"Do me one last favor," said Ángel.

"What?"

"Find out whatever you can about the woman, about Eliana. You know her address, but I'll write it down for you just in case."

Ángel wrote the address on a scrap of paper and gave it to him.

"What do you want to know?"

"Where is she now. I want to know that she's all right."

Daniel raised his voice a little.

"I'll track her down, but only so she can confess that she pulled the trigger, that's all. That's the only thing I want to hear from that bitch. She has to confess."

"No, no. Let it go."

"I'll talk to her."

"Don't do anything stupid. Don't hurt her or threaten her or anything, please. Promise."

"All right, but let me just tell you something. I've been keeping it back all this time."

"What?"

Daniel gave a sigh.

"There's good news, too. They granted you an appeal."

"Really?"

"It has to be settled in a few days. So, don't go thinking you're staying in here. The case will be heard in the Supreme Court, which has jurisdiction over the whole of Peru. The Superior Court only deals with Lima."

"That's great. Thank you. Really."

The guard was watching them. He was paying particular attention, as though he knew them.

Daniel left without so much as acknowledging him.

Over the next few nights, Ángel slept better than usual. Sometimes he managed to lie for five or six hours in his bunk without getting up, even to go to the toilet. Water was rationed, and if he drank less, he would urinate less, which was a relief for his prostate. He had to think about the advantages.

He was getting used to talking to Dimas and Sinesio. Sometimes, after lunch, they would stand in the exercise yard and chat for a while. Halfway through the morning, Ángel found himself looking forward to playing soccer. He was too old to play center forward, but as a defender or a goalkeeper, he could still intercept the ball and even make a few passes. His game improved. He became an expert at intercepting penalties, which reminded him of his achievements at school. His main technique was to keep an eye on the player taking the shot. This was something he had learned from the fighters in the ring.

In the exercise yard, the inmates would sometimes rehearse and perform in plays. Ángel once played the role of a boy's father in a family drama, something his friends found hilarious. Once, he recited a speech by Héctor Verlarde called "Hamlet in Lima" in which the prince arrived in the city and became very confused because, in Lima, "to be" and "not to be" were much the same thing.

On other occasions, there were competitions for dancing or painting. Some of the prisoners played guitar or drummed on crates. Ángel sang with the group a number of times and managed to persuade a few other inmates to sing with him. Meanwhile, his shoes and his clay figurines gradually found buyers. Dealers came by to pick them up every week.

Over time, Ángel managed to pay back the money he owed Daniel. Initially, his brother refused to take his money, but eventually Ángel convinced him that he would be doing him a favor.

One day Daniel brought in a guitar. Ángel had played when he was young, but got out of the habit after he joined the army. He could remember a few waltzes. At night, after dinner, he would go back to his block and practice before heading back to his cell. He began to remember lyrics. He would sing softly. Little by little.

One Sunday, coming out of Mass, Ángel saw father Esteban in the exercise yard. He waited until the priest had finished speaking to a group of prisoners, then slowly walked over.

"There's something I want to tell you," he said, after a moment.

"Tell me."

Ángel stared at the ground and then to one side. The yard had been scrubbed that day and there were still brush marks on the concrete. The two men, who were standing on one side of the yard, walked over to the wall and sat down. Father Esteban rested his hands in his lap. His black trousers were a little too short and hair peeked out above his socks. Ángel immediately started to speak. His voice was a taut thread. His forehead was damp with sweat.

"Listen, Esteban. I want to tell you something. It happened when I was a soldier stationed up in Ayacucho, back when the army was torturing people and taking women prisoner. Anyway, what happened was that one day the captain of my unit had a young woman tortured, she was about twenty. She had long hair and her eyes shone with a powerful light, I remember. She screamed when they strapped her to the table and as they beat her again and again, they beat her hard, they were sweating from the effort, I saw all this and I got out of there, I ran away, ran out into the countryside. I felt sick, I had to get out of there. I found my secret stash of rum and I took it to the top of a hill. I needed to be as far away as possible. I was half-dead from the cold. But I sat there. A long time passed. And all I did during that time was sit there on my own, staring up at the sky, and drinking from that bottle.

"When it was dark, I headed back. They had tortured a number of people. They'd raped the women. I saw the woman, the one I'm telling you about. She was like a rag doll. Everyone assumed she was dead. She was lying next to the other corpses in body bags. The captain asked where I'd been and, as punishment, ordered me to take her and the rest of the bodies and dump them by the roadside where the truck would come to pick them up. So, I followed his orders, I didn't try to argue. I have to admit I didn't have the strength to disobey the captain. So, I hoisted her onto my shoulder, and I could feel her warmth through the body bag, and for a moment I thought she might be alive. I moved the other corpses, but what I remember most clearly is her body slung over my shoulder. I was really drunk, and I was completely terrified, thinking that, in that moment, I'd gone insane. Insane is one way of putting it, I don't know. Then I drove to the spot, I unloaded the body bags, and as I was setting her down next to the others, the woman suddenly started to move, she got up. She was standing in front of me. I had assumed they'd killed her but there she was, alive, moving, trying to speak. She started begging me to look for her children, to help her. But I was so frightened, so shocked, that I simply raised my gun and fired. It was very dark. I saw her crumple and I ran away. I just wanted to run. When I got to the barracks, I started drinking again. I think I downed two bottles of rum. But the next day, when I realized what I'd done, I climbed to the edge of a ravine and I sat there until it got dark, I was cold and I pleaded with God to let death come and take me. All I could think about was this woman who had begged me to look for her children and how I had shot her. I was trembling with shame and rage, I hated myself, I was convinced I was going to die. I didn't go back to the barracks; in the end, they had to send out a search party. My friend, Cholo Palacios, found me lying there, my face pressed into the grass and the weeds. He carried me back to the barracks and there I stayed. And afterwards, I carried on; I did what the other soldiers were doing. I marched with them, I ate with them, I fell asleep with them, I woke up with them. I lived among them again. I followed blindly. Until I came to Lima. I left the army, and with what little I had saved in the bank and my brother's help, I bought a car. Years went by, and I worked at this and that. I ended up becoming a salesman in a store in Surquillo, and since I lived alone and wasn't happy, at night I sometimes fought at a local wrestling arena. I won some fights and lost some, but at least I could fight and punch and scream. I used to go there because it was the one place where I could scream and punch some guy, but really, I was screaming at myself. That's what I did at night. Scream and fight. Scream and fight as much as I could. But during the day I served customers. My life was spent serving customers, visiting my brother, going to the fights. Sometimes, I'd show up at work with bruises all over my face, it wasn't good for the business, but it was good for me.

"But one day something happened. The woman I shot

in Ayacucho, the woman I thought I'd killed, one day she suddenly walked into the store in Surquillo market as if it were the most normal thing in the world. Just like that. She came into the store, with her long hair and her black dress, and she asked me something. I couldn't believe it. I couldn't believe my eyes. It was definitely her. And then she asked if I'd deliver some glasses she wanted to buy to a place, a church hall, near her house. And I suddenly felt a chasm open up inside me. I don't know how to describe it. I became obsessed with the idea of seeing her again. I couldn't think about anything else. I wanted to see her, I wanted to help her, I wanted to do something for her. Like I said, it was all I could think about. I started visiting her neighborhood to look for her. I found out her name. I would go back to see her all the time. I was upsetting her. She didn't want to have anything to do with me, unsurprisingly—obviously she didn't want anything to do with me. Then one night, after a fight with some friends, when I'd had too much to drink, I went back to her house. And that night, a man I'd seen before showed up. A man who claimed to be her father. He was right there on the street, coming toward me, shouting insults and threats. I confronted him and while we were stand-ing there, the woman—Eliana her name is—she came out with a gun, she shot the man and handed me the gun. And then she disappeared. Then the police arrived and found me there."

Ángel paused. Esteban was looking at him, com-pletely still. His eyes shone with a strange light.

"And that's what's happened," Ángel went on, "that's why I'm in here, because everyone thinks I murdered him. In fact, she did it. And she gave me the gun so they'd blame me. And that's why I am here. But I'm happy here,

I don't want to change anything. It's been good for me, being in here. I've made friends. I've talked to a lot of people, and I've talked to myself too. The only thing is, I don't know what to do about what happened up in Ayacucho, I don't know what to do about her voice begging me to help, her voice pleading with me to look for her children, and sometimes I hear a gunshot, and I can see her body crumpling, or I can almost see it. It keeps coming back. I don't know what to do, because I still hear her voice, even though I'm here, paying for a crime she committed. I'm telling you that at night, when everything is quiet, her voice washes over me like a wave of fire and I feel the wave crash over my face. I'm sure a lot of other things happened in this story that I can't tell you, because I don't know them. But this was what I wanted to tell you. Forgive me, Esteban. Forgive me, but you are the only person I felt that I could tell."

Ángel fell silent. Overhead, birds fluttered, their cries cascading into the yard, a sound rarely heard inside the prison. Around them were the whitewashed bricks, the black railings, the sentry posts on towers four and six, the goalposts in the exercise yard. A damp breeze whistled along the walls.

"Thank you for telling me this, Ángel. It is always best to talk about what you're feeling. And that's what priests are here for."

Ángel carried on talking, his tone a little more shrill.

"Because that's what it is, Esteban. A voice is like a prayer. Her voice. That's what I hear. But to be honest, I almost prefer it. Because before all this happened, before I came to the prison here, I didn't feel anything. I lived like a wind-up doll, an automaton that walked and ate and talked with clients and sold glasses and crockery by day and fought in the ring by night. But I didn't feel anything. It was only when I saw her again, that first day, that I began to feel again. The day she walked into my store unannounced. But there's something I need to say, Esteban, something I need to tell you. Nothing I do will wipe away what happened that night near the barracks up in Ayacucho. That's why I want you to tell me what to do. What can I do with this shame, this rage, this self-loathing, this longing to be swallowed up by the earth, all the things I feel? I thought I'd put it all behind me, but I never forgot. Deep down, I have spent all this time wanting to die, Esteban. I still do. But I can't. I don't have the courage to die."

Ángel trailed off. He could still hear the echo of his words. A gray dust, like a blanket of ashes, seemed to be spread across the concrete. Next to the wall, a few shadows moved. Ángel saw one prisoner coming from the library with a book.

In the distance, a door opened. Family members streamed in for Sunday visiting hours. Ángel saw a man with gray hair putting his arm around a prisoner's shoulders. Esteban was looking at him.

"If you didn't kill that man, then you shouldn't be here, Ángel."

"I don't care about that. I want to talk about the other thing. About what happened there."

Esteban seemed to be recollecting something.

"I know a little about the subject," he said. "I understand what you're saying." Then, after a long silence, he added: "I don't know if I've ever mentioned that I'm from Ayacucho."

"I didn't know."

"I was there during the war. I know what you're

talking about. That's just how things were. Many women were arrested. They were abused. Nobody cared. Soldiers told them they'd get out alive."

"Did you know any of them?"

Father Esteban got up and the two men walked across the green-painted concrete pitch toward the far end of the exercise yard. They sat down on a step next to the goalpost. They were far away from passing prisoners and guards.

"Yes. Many told me their stories. People who were tortured, raped, paralyzed, left with wounds that would never heal. Their lives had been destroyed, yet they did not have the consolation of death. Men, women, even children. With no one they could turn to. They told me that the worst came later. The consequences. What they call *llakis*."

"What is that?"

The priest glanced toward the main gate.

"*Llakis* is a Quechua word for painful thoughts. Memories that stay with people. That never go away. But there is another Quechua concept they call *pampachanakuy*. The ritual of forgiveness, though it is not true forgiveness. It is a pact to ignore or set aside the actions of the past. The two parties make a pact and they bury their differences. This is how they try to deal with forgiveness. Not through confrontation, but by rising above the past. They have a phrase: Remember in order to forget. It's not like the Western concept of confrontation. It's not the same. They come together to remember so that, together, they can forget."

In the distance, a salsa rhythm drifted from a prisoner's radio.

"I'll never understand what those victims went

through," said Ángel. "I don't know how to put myself in their place. Even before the war, they lived in poverty. Not poverty as we know it, but real, abject poverty. Knowing that you might freeze to death, and having nothing to eat, knowing there is nothing you can do, and yet still doing what you can. The poverty that abandons you, alone in the universe, with nothing to wear, nothing to eat, with no hope that things might change—that's what I saw there. How can anyone live with such poverty, Esteban, and with no hope? Tell me."

"I think it's possible to live with poverty, but not without hope."

"I'm not sure."

"And when you are forced to watch as those you love die—that's something I cannot understand. There's a Quechua word, *waqcha*, it means "orphan." But it also means "poverty." Poverty and death. The death of those you love most. To suddenly have to carry on without your family is very different from what you might imagine. It's something the mind cannot take on. So many were left without parents, without brothers and sisters, without children. Families they might have lived with for years to come, but for the war. Why did all this have to happen? Why did it have to be that way? Why did they have to be so poor, why did they have to watch their parents, their children, die? The friends I knew up in Ayacucho used to say that life there could have been different. It would have been different, if they had not lost their families. Of course, it would have been different. But being the poorest of the poor, they were also the most vulnerable. They had no way to defend themselves. They were living in little towns and villages with barely enough to survive. With nothing to eat but beans and fruit, and precious little to keep them warm. And then the war came. First came Shining Path, and then the soldiers. Violence from both sides, though the terrorists were even more brutal, I'd say. But there was also this other brutality: the poverty, the disease, the cold, the lack of help, of doctors, of everything, a brutality that they had known their whole lives. It is something that we cannot understand, but they can. And some of them fight back. They work, they do what they can to earn money, they try and live with what friends and family they have left, try to celebrate holidays and birthdays because they know there is no reason for them to be poor, no reason for them to die so young. And that's true. I once watched a group of villagers carry a pregnant woman through the Ayacucho jungle to the hospital in Andahuaylas. There was nowhere in Ayacucho that could treat her. And so they carried her though the night. Along the way, the woman delivered her baby and it was choked by the umbilical cord, and still they continued walking, carrying her and her dead child through jungle and mountains, until they reached the hospital at Andahuaylas. They had been walking for twenty-four hours. Only there, in the hospital, was there anyone who could treat her. It's something that happens all the time. Everyone who lives there knows that. There are not stories about it in the newspapers, but it happens all the time. I went to Andahuaylas and talked to the woman while she was recovering. She was devastated, naturally. Then, suddenly, she said that in spite of everything she still believed in God. Even now. This astonishes me, and it reinforces my faith. It helps me to believe, but it also fills me with rage. . . . It fills me with rage, but I choke it back. I'm saying it aloud so everyone can hear—even God."

Father Esteban was looking at him with a strangely serene expression. Ángel's lips had begun to curve into a smile, but the smile drained away. He bowed his head, then looked at the priest again.

"What can I do, Esteban? I feel happier here than I am out there, but I still find it difficult to carry on living."

"The first thing you need to do is forgive yourself. I don't know how. It's very difficult. But you have to do something. Work to forgive yourself. Help somebody. Do something for someone else. If you've done somebody harm, and you cannot fix it, do something good. I don't know. Honestly, it's difficult to give advice. Help those people as you can. People you know, those who need help. Maybe that's the best way."

"The one thing I will not do is forget. I couldn't, even if I wanted to."

"Of course not, Ángel. You can't forget what happened. And you should not forget her. In the end, I don't think it's about forgetting or even forgiving, it's something else. It's about living with pain and turning it into a force that helps others. A man cannot forgive himself for something like this. But he can try and become a different man. Do it through work, through helping people. Besides, to forgive yourself does not mean to forget. It is a way of remembering the evil that you did but ensuring that it means something. Sometimes, though, I'm not sure I understand it either."

"But what can I do?"

"That's up to you. Help all the people you can, like I said. And keep talking to yourself."

Two boys appeared in the exercise yard. They were Sinesio's sons.

"And maybe talk to her, if I can."

"You should feel that you can talk to her, can look her in the eye, even though you are alone."

"I'd like to track her down. And say something to her."

"I thought you said she doesn't want to see you?"

Father Esteban was looking at him. He had a deep furrow on his brow.

"You don't think I should look for her?"

"I can't answer that. But, from what you've said, it's clear that she doesn't want to see you. You can't carry on obsessively looking for her. One day, you'll get out of here, but even then, it would be better to wait a while."

"It's about confronting the past. Something I've never been good at. It would be better to forget."

They sat in silence. A breeze ruffled Esteban's hair.

"The past is not what has happened, you know," the priest said. "The past is what will happen."

A ward emerged from an office door on the far side of the yard and gestured to Esteban. They were waiting for him.

"What do you mean?"

"Time, in Andean culture, is perceived differently to the way it is in Western culture. The Quechua word *ñawpa* means "past," but it also means "forward.""

"So, the past is what lies ahead? Is that what you mean?"

"The past lies ahead of us because we already know it. The future lies behind us because it is still unknown. The word *yuyay* means "to think" but also "to remember." In Quechua, memory and knowledge are synonymous. This is something we need to learn: to face our past. Only there will you find a way to forgive yourself, if you can. But you do it to channel your guilt into something useful, if only to help you live a better life with those around you. You knew all this already, you simply forgot it for a while."

Father Esteban's voice was measured, as though he had spent a long time thinking about these words. In that moment, his eyes were shining, huge and liquid. Something about his expression had changed. At times, he reminded Ángel of Eliana.

Esteban got to his feet. The yard was almost empty now.

"I've got to go now, but we can talk again whenever you want."

Ángel nodded.

"Thank you," he said.

He watched as Esteban disappeared into a group of people.

In the days that followed, Ángel devoted more time to his clay figurines. Obsessed with certain figures, he began to visit different workshops. One day, he painted a portrait of a woman, dark-skinned, willowy, with long hair. She looked nothing like Eliana. Then he painted another of himself, strolling next to her. In another, he and his imaginary partner were in a field strewn with flowers. In another workshop, he embroidered these same figures onto fabric. At first, he depicted them as part of a crowd. Later, he whittled down the crowd until only they remained, but he separated the couple, placing one on a hill in the top left corner and the other in the bottom right with empty space between. With each new piece, he moved them closer together, adjusted the subtle lines of their bodies, their faces. Over time, they felt closer to each other.

During this time, there was building work going on

in one of the blocks. Laborers showed up with bags of cement, girders, bricks, a few piles of sand. Ángel contemplated the mound of sand: this was the time that had passed, time reduced to a heap of tiny grains. The air was filled with dust, a thick curtain he had to pass through to cross the exercise yard.

But he could not carry on overthinking everything. He felt such satisfaction when he finished a figurine that all he wanted was to start on another. Working with his hands, creating something physical, persuading himself that no one but him could have made it . . . he felt new blood coursing through his body. Every morning he went jogging and did exercises. He realized that he had lost weight.

At lunchtime, he would find his friends and chat. He looked forward to Daniel's Sunday visits. He was in prison and he felt happy. Two years had passed.

One morning, his brother Daniel arrived earlier than usual. They met in the visitors' yard. Daniel took a seat opposite him and set down a bag from which he extracted several magazines.

Suddenly he said:

"I went looking for her."

"You did?"

The day before, Daniel had showed up at Eliana's house after work.

"I rang the doorbell a couple of times. Eventually, as I was about to leave, a woman with a long face appeared at the door. She looked at me suspiciously . . .

"I want to speak to Eliana," I said.

"Who's Eliana?"

"Doesn't she live here?"

"No. The previous owners sold the house and we don't know nothing about them."

"You don't know where they went?"

"I don't know nothing. Why are you looking for her?"

"It's personal."

The woman turned. She began to close her door.

"Tell me, Señora," said Daniel. "You don't happen to know the previous owners' address?"

Through the gap in the door, the woman's voice sounded hoarse and sinister.

"No. We don't know nothing. It was a long time ago. We don't know nothing about none of them. Can't even remember their names."

"But I asked around the neighborhood," Daniel went on, "and I searched through the records of an organization called Ideele. I went to their offices, and they let me use a computer to search their records. And I found a mention of her."

Daniel stared at his brother. There were more wrinkles around his eyes now.

"Eliana Cauti, her name is."

"I already knew that."

"You knew? That's great. Good of you to share. So, why is the father's surname Huarón?"

"I'm not convinced he was her father. What else did you find out?"

Daniel threw up his hands in despair. A few columns surrounded the yard attached to the block. In the distance were the goal posts, a mural on the wall, two public telephones, and tables where other prisoners were sitting, talking to their families.

"It's a pretty fucked-up story," he went on. "She was found one day wandering along a road covered in dirt and blood. Some farmers took her back to their house. She was badly injured. But alive."

"And?"

"According to the statements, as soon as she recovered, she caught a bus and went looking for her children. The bus took her to Lima. That's when she showed up at Señor Huarón's house. That's where the witness statements end. They say it's not clear what happened after that. But I know."

"She moved in with him?"

"Yeah. The neighbors who run the bodega told me what happened. I had to buy everything they had to get them to tell me."

Daniel swung his legs from side to side.

"And?"

Just then, the two men heard shouts coming from the other side of the wall. Ángel could hear an excitable voice commenting on a soccer match on the radio. Daniel talked over the chatter. He spoke softly, but so clearly that it seemed as though his voice were the only sound.

"What happened between her and Huarón is this: during the war, on the day she managed to get away, Huarón saw her on Calle Tres Máscaras in Ayacucho, banging on the door of a house. He called over, asked her what was wrong. She said she was looking for her family. He persuaded her to come to his house, which was close by. He took her up to his room. He tended to her wounds. Even took her to see a doctor. After a few days in Huarón's house she had more or less recovered. But every time she woke, she asked for her children. And so Huarón promised to find her children if she worked for him and tended to his sexual needs. That's how he put it. If she tended to his sexual needs, he'd look for her children. He had connections; he would be able to find them. I've no idea whether what these people told me is true. If you want to know what I think, I can't understand how people can be so evil."

Daniel lit a cigarette. He spoke through the blue, evanescent whorls.

"You're not allowed to smoke here," one of the guards growled.

"I know," Daniel said. "But what are you going to do, lock me up?"

"I don't know how you managed to get these cigarettes through security, Señor," said the guard.

Daniel made a face and stubbed out his cigarette.

"So, tell me. What actually happened between her and Huarón?"

"Everything, pretty much."

"What?"

"Huarón tormented her, he promised he'd help find her children, but in return she had to sleep with him. He used this story to drag her here to Lima, apparently. When she finally realized he was lying to her, she ran away with the help of some cousins who lived in Lima. She joined a religious group and tried to forget the whole thing. Some years passed. But then Huarón tracked her down, he got a house on the same street. He hounded her. He was constantly stalking her. That's when you showed up."

Daniel fell silent. The sounds from the other side of the wall had faded. Some of the inmates had gone back into the block.

Ángel felt a surge of joy. All things considered, it was good that Huarón was dead. He was glad that he had been charged with the crime. He was happy for people to think that he was the one who had murdered him.

"So, anyway, that's the story," Daniel went on. "But no one knows where Eliana might be now. Wherever she is, she's better off without that guy making her life hell. And she's free. Thanks to you."

"I know, but there's something else. There's something else."

Daniel looked at him gravely.

"I don't know what else there could be. The important thing now is to get you out of here, *hermano*."

"Don't worry about me. I've got everything I need in here. And I've got friends."

"In here, you're alone with your thoughts, and that's all you care about, you don't give a shit about the rest of us."

Daniel's sudden outburst echoed loudly around the walls of the exercise yard. The guards and some of the other prisoners turned to look. There was a long silence.

"It's more complicated than you think, Daniel."

"Why?"

Ángel nodded at his photograph.

"Because of her."

"What has Mamá got to do with this? She died years ago."

"I know. We could have had more time with her."

"For most of our lives, Mamá wasn't around. And then she died. That's that. That's all there is to it. Don't fuck around."

"Things could have been different for her. And for us."

"But they weren't, were they?" Daniel said, watching a cat slink between the tables. "We spent as much time as we could with her, and we can't change the past. We have to accept it."

"We can change the past. We need to think about what happened, truly think about it."

Daniel sat in silence. A water pump had juddered into life. It rumbled inside the walls.

"Sometimes people leave you and they don't come back," he said. "That's life. That's all there is to it. We have nothing to feel guilty about, do we?"

Ángel's lips moved. He was muttering something.

"And you haven't heard from Papá?"

Daniel pulled a face.

"We never talk about Papá, you know that. He would poison our mouths."

A fly fluttered into the yard and began buzzing around Ángel before landing on Daniel's hand.

"Fucking bug," Daniel said, shaking it off.

"Things could have been different," Ángel said. "They didn't have to be the way they were."

"Why are you so obsessed with this shit?"

"If we're free to do as we please, then we're guilty too, that's what I believe. What I mean is, we can't go around living like animals, without realizing the cost of the things we do."

"We'll always be guilty, Ángel. That's what you're saying. We'll always be to blame for something. Bad things happen around us, and not because of something we've done. But it's normal to feel guilty. We're born prepared to shoulder blame. It's a part of us. Listen, *hermano*, I'm fifty years old, you're forty-five. We've both had friends and relatives who died. They're dead. That's life. There's nothing more to be said, we just have to let them go. For you, for me, the fact that we're still alive is a privilege.

But the fact that others are dead is nobody's fault. Are we responsible for those who died? The problem is that you torment yourself. You latch onto guilt and you cling to it to the bitter end. You shoulder the blame for evil things that others have done, you spend your life obsessing about it. That's what you do, Ángel. But what good does it do you, Ángel, tell me?"

"I'm not talking about other people, Daniel. *I* did something evil."

"So what? We've all done bad things. Terrible things. We didn't mean to, but we did. That's how things go. We do our best not to make the same mistakes twice. Are we supposed to lie down and die because of it? There are people all around us, asshole. We can't spend our lives continually whining to them about our fucking suffering, or maybe you want to carry on like this forever?"

Ángel gave a sad smile, as though he understood his brother better than he thought.

The exercise yard was almost deserted now. Visitors had begun to leave. Another silence settled over them.

There was hardly a sound.

"Sometimes I think that death is just a place you pass through. The dead should be able to come back now and then. You die, you go away, but from time to time you come back. The dead should visit, talk to people, make sure things are in order, and then leave again. An occasional visit, until next time. That's how it should be with the dead," Ángel said.

In the distance, they heard an unexpected burst of salsa music. It was coming from one of the cells.

"We have to set everything to music and just keep on keeping on," Daniel said. "We have our friends, our family. There's far too much shit in the world to be going around worrying about dead people and people we don't even know. We should be concerned about those we know, those we love. Not the others. There's nothing we can do for them. They left us, and that's all there is to say."

Ángel raised his voice.

"Well, fuck that, because I believe we should remember them," he said. "I believe we need to think about the other people, even people we don't know. Each thought about another person can help us live better lives. It might even help to make this world a little less shitty. Do you think that's ridiculous?"

"You and your ideas. You're just like Mamá. That's how she was. Always kind. Always chatting to people, always with a kind word for people, even if she didn't know them."

"She thought about other people," said Ángel.

"And what good did it do her?"

"You always ask what good things do. Being kind does a lot of good."

"I don't see how."

"When we're kind to someone, to some random stranger, it makes the world a slightly better place, Daniel. And that's good for everyone, even if you don't see it. A friend once told me he'd spent a long time thinking about killing some guy. He had it all planned. He was going to go around to the guy's house and shoot him because of something the guy had done to him. But on the day he planned to kill him, he stopped off at a newsstand because he was nervous and he was dying of thirst. When he realized he didn't have enough money, the woman gave him a bottle for whatever change he had. Just drink it, he told me she said. He drained the whole bottle. And maybe you won't believe this, but because of that, because of that woman's gesture, he decided that maybe that guy didn't deserve to die, that maybe he shouldn't be doing this shit. So, rather than kill him, he simply never saw the guy again. He didn't go through with it. He didn't kill the man. The funniest thing is that the other guy never knew he owed his life to a woman at a newsstand."

"What's that got to do with us?"

"I don't know. Maybe nothing. But an act of kindness can sometimes save one life, or even many, I don't know. You can trigger a domino effect. Your casual greeting to a stranger might mean something, might mean a lot to the person on the receiving end, who knows?"

"I don't get it. This is just mind games. That's not how I think. But maybe . . ."

Ángel interrupted.

"Eliana asked me to look for her children. They were alive back then."

"Will you forget about that woman, for fuck's sake? Focus on the people you know, asshole. Think about my children, for example. My children love you. They're your family. And here you are thinking about anyone but them. About some woman you don't even know. But my children are your family, asshole."

"And I want to see them too."

Ángel trailed off. He felt tears well up. There were times when he had felt ashamed at what his niece and nephew must think of him.

"But don't bring them here," he said. "I don't want them to see me like this."

There was a long silence. The shadow of the watch-tower grew longer. A cockroach scuttled along a windowsill.

"I think I did know the woman from before," Ángel said at length. His voice sounded livelier, as though it belonged to a younger man. "I figured out that I used to know her. I don't know from when, probably when we were young and living in Ayacucho. I met her before. I know that now."

"Fine, but no one knows where she is now. You did her this favor, you took the blame for killing that son of a bitch, and she got away scot-free."

Ángel's breathing was labored. There was no point talking to his brother about this anymore, he thought. He felt exhausted and his legs ached, as though he had been walking for a long time.

Daniel took a sweater from his bag.

"Here. Winter is drawing in. Maybe if you wrap up warm, your thoughts won't be so gloomy, compadre."

He looked at his watch.

"Listen, I have to go, I'm meeting up with the family."

"Sure."

Daniel got to his feet.

"Bye, Ángel. See you Sunday."

"Thanks, Daniel. I mean that."

"Oh, I nearly forgot. I fired Longo. Poor bastard. I'll send a new lawyer. You'll see."

Ángel watched as his brother walked away. He wanted to run after him, thank him again, but stopped himself. Only then did it occur to him that his brother had put on weight.

That night, Ángel lay down with his two photographs.

"What do you think?" he said to his mother. "What do you think? Turns out I killed the bastard who was making her life hell. I did a good thing, didn't I? You should be proud of me."

He turned to the other photograph.

"I feel better now."

Without warning, Ángel became lost in shadows. For a split-second, he felt as though the clouds were a flock of sinister sheep scudding across the white sky. Suddenly he found himself flying over a valley, he saw a river, its banks thick with yellow elder. Eliana was standing on the bank. She came toward him. Her two young children were with her, they stretched their arms toward him. Eliana said they should set off. They were going to go for a walk. A moment later, they were running with the children through meadows, laughing. Fleetingly, he saw their faces. They were the faces of Daniel's children, Jorge and Vanessa, his niece and nephew, a few years earlier.

He woke, walked over to the barred window, and stared out at the foggy exercise yard punctured by points of light. The world vaguely sketched itself in the outlines of the building, the remoteness of the rooftops, the outcrops of the water tanks, a halo of clouds ringing the moon. He stood there, gazing out. Feeling Eliana's hand in his as they ran.

The following day, Ángel was informed that he had a visitor. He went to the narrow room with its tables and chairs. He saw the motto "You are the architect of your own destiny," and smiled.

Standing next to the nearest table, a thin man with a briefcase was waiting. He was wearing a dark coat, corduroy pants, and a shiny, gray jacket. He was scrawny and his hair was disheveled from the vagaries of the morning.

The briefcase swinging in his hand seemed to have a life of its own.

"Señor Ángel Serpa?"

"Yes."

The man smiled, looking him up and down. His voice was brisk and clear.

"Just one question, Señor Serpa. Tell me something. Every guilty man dreams of getting out of here. You're innocent, but you don't want to leave. Why is that?"

"Who are you, Señor?"

The man handed him a card.

"Alfredo Sánchez Griñán, attorney. Your attorney from now on. Your brother Daniel sent me."

"Oh, I see . . ."

Sánchez Griñán took a seat. He looked Ángel in the eye. Ángel sat next to him.

"Let me tell you something, Señor Serpa. The one thing this profession has taught me is that you never learn anything. No sooner do you come to a conclusion than something comes along to disprove it. Attorneys work with people, and people are unpredictable. We're constantly surprised. In a nutshell, to be an attorney is to be constantly surprised. Though I suppose you could say that about any profession. But my profession is all about surprises, take my word for it."

One by one, he took out a series of documents.

Sánchez Griñán shook his head several times.

"Your brother has told me what happened," he told Ángel. "We're going to get you out of here, but you have to cooperate."

"If you say so."

"We are going to put together a new case file for the appeal."

Ángel looked down.

"All right, if you say so."

"For God's sake, show a little enthusiasm. And pay attention."

"I'm paying attention."

Ángel looked into the man's calm, piercing eyes. The attorney had come with a prepared speech.

"I know that you know who murdered Señor Huarón, but you don't want to say anything." He held up his hand. "Don't even try and deny it. I'm sure you have your reasons for not telling the truth. The truth is a very complicated thing. What I will say is that I only partly understand your case. The part I don't yet understand is not helpful. The important thing is that we're going to get you out of here, so sort yourself out."

Ángel was grateful for the attorney's volubility.

"If you say so," he said.

Dimas Donayre walked past. He was also meeting with his attorney.

"We'll see whether this one's any good," he said as he passed.

"Would you like me to get you some water?" Ángel politely offered. Being in prison, it felt amusing to play the gracious host.

"No, thank you," the attorney said.

Sánchez Griñán was holding a manila folder.

"This is the account of your arrest," he said. "It's full of contradictions. . . . You're lucky the officers were so inept. They were obviously in a hurry to clock off that night. They didn't even bother to do a gunshot residue test. And you were clearly confused at the time."

"Maybe so. But my brother should have talked to me before hiring a new lawyer. No offense."

Sánchez Griñán took another folder from his briefcase.

"He told me you knew. Don't worry about that now. Let's press on, Señor Ángel."

The attorney's expression was shrewd and determined.

Ángel felt as though he could trust this man. There was something so frank and sincere about his face that it felt like a visit from a friend whose existence he was unaware of until now.

"All right."

"Don't worry. You'll be better off with me."

"If you say so . . ."

"We will take the appeal all the way to the Supreme Court. We are going to make the strongest possible case."

"Okay."

"But you have to cooperate, Señor Serpa. Don't you want to be released?"

"Sometimes I feel happy doing what I do in here."

The attorney set down the documents and looked at Ángel. His face was tense. Ángel realized that his brother had told him everything about Eliana.

"No, Señor Serpa. You don't feel happy. You want to stay here because you're afraid of being out there, that's all."

"I don't know. I see you know everything about me."

"Listen, I'm going to tell you something: I understand you. I genuinely understand you."

"I don't know why you would say that."

The attorney smiled.

"The fact is, when we're young we make lots of mistakes, Señor Serpa. And when we grow up, what happens? We carry on screwing things up. And as we grow old, we're still making mistakes, sometimes worse ones. Fundamentally, human beings never learn. We're factories that churn out mistakes. Why? Because we isolate ourselves. Because it seems easier to do things on our own. Because we're afraid. That's just the way it is. That's why we make mistakes. People sometimes regret mistakes they've made, but what good is that when they carry on making them? But sometimes people do good things. That's the interesting part. Sometimes the noble deeds and the mistakes are part of the same story. Obviously, I'm including myself in what I've said. I'm like everyone else."

"I don't know who I am anymore," said Ángel.

"Of course you do, Señor Ángel. You're not a fool, only perhaps a little naïve, and I say that with the utmost respect. You want to be a good man. Like most people. And why do people do noble things? For the same reasons people make mistakes. For the same reasons people do evil things. Because they let themselves be led by their imagination. People rarely have a sense of reality. They spend their time thinking about the castles they build in the clouds rather than the ground they're walking on. And there is something magical about that, I think. Something admirable, but it can also lead to a terrible catastrophe. That's what I've learned from years of practicing law. You've got your problems, Señor Ángel. But better to have those problems out in the world than in here. There's more to do out there. In winter, you can go for coffee in the café on the corner, in summer you can walk along the seafront. They're simple things, but pleasurable. Don't you think? You could do them. The rest is all bullshit— and I say that with the utmost respect, as you know."

The attorney gazed at him. Ángel felt the impulse to smile.

"Maybe . . . ," he said.

Sánchez Griñán nodded to the folder on the table.

"This is the appeal we're going to file. There's also a copy of the police report from that first night at the police station. We're going to draw up a list of points in your favor."

"I can't think what those could be."

"First, we know from the angle of the gunshot that the bullet was fired by somebody who was right-handed. And you're left-handed. Your brother told me. So, that's a point we can include."

Ángel shrugged.

"That's true."

"On the night you were arrested, you made statements that no one understood. There was no confession, in the strict sense. You contradicted yourself in your statements. Initially, you said there was a struggle. Then you said you saw a man running away. There isn't simply one statement, there are two, because in court you said something completely different. Then there's the fact that no paraffin test was carried out for gunshot residue. The officers forgot. It's unbelievable. I am going to ask for your sentence to be reviewed and put together a new defense."

"Very good."

"I'm only going to ask you for one thing: cheer up. You'll hear about what I'm doing."

Sánchez Griñán slipped the folder back in his briefcase.

"Thank you," said Ángel.

"There's no need to thank me. Trust me, from what I know about you, I genuinely understand you. Better than you think."

The attorney walked toward the exit. For the first time in a long while, Ángel felt the urge to follow somebody out into the street.

In the following months, Ángel had numerous visits from Sánchez Griñán. They met in the visiting room filled with tables and chairs. Often, Sánchez Griñán came bearing good news. He had taken the necessary legal steps and was hopeful that the appeal would be heard quickly. The appeal was steadily scaling the hills of the judicial system, like a "determined mountaineer," as he once put it, steadily gaining new ground in ever-steeper terrain. One day, you'll make it to the summit, Sinesio told him. Ángel felt cheered not so much by the news but by the attorney's enthusiasm.

During this period, he made some new friends. One of them was moved into his cell, to the bunk opposite his.

His name was Salvador Ponciano, and he was in for attempted murder. He was a gray-haired, tight-lipped man with mournful eyes. He had shot a friend during a fight. He and the victim had been drinking into the early hours. At 6 a.m., Salvador Ponciano had said he was heading home to bed. His friend started insulting him. You're a fucking asshole, stay here and drink with me! He accused Salvador of not being able to hold his drink. Then he started laying into his wife. He said terrible things about her. It was at that point that Salvador took out his gun and shot him. As his friend crumpled, he had smiled, perhaps a smile of triumph. He had achieved something he had always longed for: he could blame Salvador for something. But he didn't die. Salvador still thought of him as a friend; in fact, he cared more about him now. At night, he prayed to him, and to his saints. These things happen, he had said to his friend. But why did you have to insult me like that? And why did you insult my wife?

Conversations in prison are different from those that people have when they're free, Ángel thought. In prison, conversations have greater value. The thought that they will never be released is something that unites people in here. Every word is the last. Even the sky looks different when seen from the exercise yard. It's more beautiful.

In the afternoons, during the prisoners' free time, Salvador Ponciano would come over and try to tell Ángel his life story. Some nights, Ángel heard him sobbing quietly.

One day, he admitted the truth. The friend he had shot had slept with Salvador's wife. So he had reached for his gun. He had shot someone he had always cared about.

Ever since, he had felt constant remorse, but he had a "just conscience," he said. Ángel was not sure what he meant by the phrase, but he thought it pointless to ask.

One morning Ángel got to talking with one of the prison guards.

Dionisio Zamora had spent twenty years working there. His broad, pudgy body propped up the black mole on his nose. Someone had described his body as three stacked potatoes with a fly stuck to the top one. Dionisio had the voice of a penniless soprano with a cold, which often led him to say that his voice was only a few tones lower than a pig's squeal. Ángel was not sure exactly what the phrase was supposed to mean, but it sounded accurate.

When he had first started, Dionisio Zamora had spent time guarding the front gate before being transferred to office work and later to supervising prisoners in the exercise yard. What he most enjoyed was wandering through the prison, chatting with the inmates.

"Those little animal figurines you make are really nice," he said, coming into the workshop.

"I've made bulls, dogs, and horses. Now, every morning when I wake up all I think about is making more."

During his time there, Zamora had made friends

with many prisoners. He had seen some of them die from sheer boredom and despair. Sometimes they went for lunch, then went to take a nap and never woke up, he said. It was pretty common. They died from a heart attack or whatever. But actually, they died from worry or from grief. They died of loneliness. When they died, it was always said, from now on they won't be sleeping here at night, they'll be dreaming all day and all night. That's how it goes. Sometimes a life filled with joy, with pain, with hope ends with a dumb joke. That's the funniest thing.

"The only thing prisoners are interested in is how their case is going and when they'll be released," he said. "But given the judicial system in this country, most of them will die waiting, which is a good way to die, if you think about it. You die in hope."

"What about you?" Ángel asked.

"I'm happy working here. I enjoy waking up, coming to the prison, and seeing you all. I'm always making friends with prisoners. I'm sad when I go home at night. Me and my wife don't get on. And the children all moved out a long time ago."

Dionisio had learned a lot from the prisoners. One had taught him to work leather; another, the basics of carpentry. After all, we're all in prison, he would say philosophically, whether you're in here or out there. It's just that the dumb schmucks out there think they're free. At least you lot know where you stand.

"You talk such shit," Dimas Donayre would say, with a smile. "You think you're so intelligent because you spout more shit than anyone else."

"What you don't realize, Dimas," Salvador said, "is that most people go through life without anyone even noticing. Prison is the only refuge for artists who want to make their mark."

"You're always adding crazy shit to your repertoire," Dimas said, smiling. "At least it's fun listening to you. What's next?"

"And what would you know, asshole?"

Sometimes Dionisio would interrupt to change the subject. Butting in on the prisoners' conversations was something he enjoyed. They were his closest friends. This was why Dionisio always showed up early for his shift and stayed late chatting with the inmates.

One day he showed up with the news that his wife had left him. She had gone to live with her sister. She had left a note. "Gone to my sister's. Don't come looking for me. You can keep the house." That was all. Fucking bitch.

There was only room for a single thought, Dionisio went on. Thirty years of marriage had been ended by a scant few words. "Gone to my sister's. Don't come looking for me." When you marry, you say: "I do." When you separate, you say: "Gone to my sister's." Her sister's even skinnier than she is, he added. Well, they'll both get a lot skinnier because I won't be sending them any money. Bitch. Walking out on me . . . but I'll make her pay, you wait and see. I'll make the bitch pay.

From that day onward, he admitted, he was resigned to being alone. I'll never be with any woman again. Unless she happens to be the woman of my dreams.

The truth was that, looking like a stack of potatoes, with a black mole and baffled toad-like eyes, Dionisio would find it tough to win over the woman of his dreams. He often talked about his ideal woman. Tall, slim, blond, green eyes. That's how I like them. But on the pittance he earned, he'd say, all he could afford were whores as ugly as he was. But he loved his little whores. Loved all of them. He even pitied some of them.

"Once, when I was young, I had to choose between a woman I loved and a woman I pitied," he admitted to Dimas, Ángel, and Salvador in the visiting room. "And fuck it, I chose the woman I pitied."

"Really?"

"And d'you know why?" he said, raising his index finger. "I'll tell you why. Because pity is the most powerful human emotion there is."

He raised his glass.

"To pity," he said.

"Gotta drink to something," Dimas said, raising his glass. "Might as well be this guy's bullshit."

That night, Ángel heard his mother's voice. She was standing by his bed, telling him the story of a placid lake where the people of Huanta used to go to relax. It was in Rasuhuilca, less than ten miles outside the city. The surface of the water was blue-green. Nearby were other smaller lakes. The townspeople depended on these, since they provided water for the town and for irrigating the crops.

But everyone in Huanta knew that, at the bottom of the lake, there lurked a ferocious animal. A bull, deep below the surface, charging from one bank to the other. The beast that troubled the waters had always longed to break free. It was prevented only by a snare fashioned by an old crone from her long hair. One day the bull managed to break its bonds, burst free of the net of hair, and appear at the surface. The waters of the lake heaved and churned and flooded the city. The townspeople were then forced to recapture the beast and drag it back to the bottom of the lake, hoping it would never again escape. But the bull was just waiting for another chance.

Ángel woke in the middle of the night. He drew the curtain. His three cellmates were sleeping. Then he saw the bull floating above him. He leaned closer. He touched its hide, felt its wet nose, and heard it bellow. He saw the water churning. He heard his mother's voice telling the end of the story and himself pleading with her to tell it again. He sat on his bunk and waited for his mother to return the bull to the lake. He realized it was a figure he had made many times, a clay bull that he painstakingly painted black. Every time he sold one of those pieces, he was sharing his dream.

After a while, he heaved a sigh of relief. He looked out the window. There was nothing. Only the prisoners' clothes hanging on the line, like countless flags fluttering in the mist.

Over the next few weeks, Sánchez Griñán's visits became more frequent.

The situation had gradually become clearer, he explained. The judge had granted the appeal. This was unsurprising, since the ballistics report was unambiguous. The bullet that had killed Eliana's so-called father, shattering his sternum, had been fired by someone who was right-handed. Everyone knows the sternum is the most vulnerable part of the body, the attorney went on, because when it shatters, bone particles rip through the internal organs. Whoever fired the gun knew exactly what they were doing. To kill someone, you have to aim for the third shirt button, this is something all cops and criminals know. It's worth keeping in mind, because you never know who you might want to kill, maybe when you least expect it. But my client was a simple salesman—how would he have known?

It is an unarguable fact that the bullet was fired from somewhere to the right of the victim, near the entry wound, your honor. This makes the charges against the defendant difficult, indeed impossible, to sustain, given that Señor Ángel Serpa is left-handed. How could his previous defense attorney have missed this fact?

"Longo was a pompous man, but that was all," Dionisio Zamora said one day. "You're better off with your new lawyer. The chances are good now that the case is in a different court."

"The opening statement for the defense should be enough," Daniel said. "There's no evidence. And besides, everyone knows you're innocent."

"Besides, no one liked Huarón, and some people even thought he was murdered as payoff for his debts," Zamora said.

"Or as revenge for one of the many women he had abused," Dimas Donayre said. "There are lots of reasons for murdering someone. That's the only thing I've learned. Who would we like to see dead? That's a secret we all share. But we hardly ever say it aloud. You tell me who you want dead and I'll tell you. But you'd be better off not telling me."

The next morning, Ángel waited for Salvador Ponciano to tell him what was happening with his case. But Salvador did not show up for breakfast. When the guards checked his cell, they found him lying on his bunk, a lifeless mass. His face was ashen, his eyes swollen. He was barely moving.

Ángel stepped closer. Salvador suddenly opened his eyes and stared at Ángel. He could scarcely move his lips. He spoke in a whisper. "I hardly slept a wink all night, compadre. I've got a pain here, feels like my chest is being ripped apart, a terrible pain. I don't know what's going on. It feels like a vise crushing my chest, and I've got shooting pains down my arms, I've never felt anything like it."

Dionisio Zamora appeared.

"I'll go fetch a medic," he said.

Salvador lay on the bed, barely breathing. His eyes had a frozen gleam.

"Don't worry," Ángel said. "The medic will be here any minute."

Salvador was shaking his head.

"All the dumb fucking shit I've done!" he muttered.

"Don't think about that now."

"Can I ask you a favor, compadre?"

"Sure."

"Take my hand, compadre. Squeeze my hand and keep me company. I want someone with me when I die."

Ángel took his hand.

"Don't talk rubbish, Salvador. The medic will be here any minute."

"I'm being serious. All the dumb things I've done."

"Cough, compadre. You have to cough. Cough as much as you can."

Salvador began to cough and sob and cough, and then he lay still, one hand covering his tear-stained face in shame. Ángel held his other hand and kept telling him: "You're going to be fine, compadre, don't worry, just cough and breathe."

"I can die in peace now. For all the stupid shit I've

done, at least I had you as a friend. What happened with my wife, compadre? Jesus fuck."

Ángel lifted up Salvador's feet and propped them on bricks. Suddenly Dimas appeared with an aspirin. Salvador swallowed it and seemed calmer. Then he began to sob again.

Ángel felt curiously serene. He shifted closer. Laid a hand on his shoulder.

"Listen to me, compadre," Ángel said. "You have to stick around. You can't leave me in here alone. I couldn't bear to be alone in this place, it would be a nightmare. Even if everything is shit, you have to hold it together, have to pull through. You have to fight back, do you understand? Get through it as best you can . . . but it's something no one can get through alone. We all have to do it together. I can talk to you. We're the same, you and me. Hell, you're as dumb as I am. You're as sick and tired as I am. You don't know how to do anything, same as me. You get excited about anything. We're each as fucked up as the other. That's why we get along so well. That's why we're friends. I can't stand all those people walking around out there who are better than me, better than us. They know where they're going, they get to go home, they have something to eat, someone to hold. They're not alone. You and me, we're alone. Maybe that's our fault. But it's also why we're friends. So that we're not alone anymore. So that we're not nothing. Or to put it another way, maybe we are trash, but at least we realize it. And we can admit it to each other. And we're together. We're brothers, compadre. We have breakfast together, we shit, we work, we're banged up together. Here we are, and that's the way it is. Here we are. It's funny, but what can we do? Well, I'll tell you what we're going to do. I tell you what I'm thinking and how I'm feeling, and you can tell me. When I see you, I know I can talk to you. If I manage to get through being in here, it will be because of our conversations, compadre. If you leave, who am I going to talk to? You can't leave. I need you, compadre. I need someone to share all this shit with. Better to have friends in here than to be alone out there. I really believe that. Can you hear me? I need you with me. You can't leave, because if you do, I'll be alone in here and I'll be fucked. That's the truth, compadre, that's it and that's all."

Ángel trailed off. Salvador was smiling, but he wasn't moving. There was no sign of the medic.

"But I've done so many dumb things and there's no way to fix them now," he murmured, trying to hold back tears.

Salvador's outstretched legs twitched from side to side.

"Being alive means doing dumb things. Or doing anything. But you still have to try and live as best you can. Even if the life we have is in here."

Salvador's skin was lined with wrinkles. His hands were pale from being squeezed together so tightly. Suddenly he turned to look at Ángel.

At that moment, the door opened. It was Dionisio, and next to him was a medic and two nurses with a stretcher. The doctor was squat, wore a white coat, and barked orders like a tinpot general.

"We have to move him," he said. "He can't stay here."

Ángel watched as Salvador was carried out on a stretcher. Watched as the door closed and realized that it might be the last time he would ever see his friend.

Later, he found out that Salvador had been transferred

to the Dos de Mayo hospital. Dionisio came by that evening with the news. Salvador was in surgery.

The next day, in the exercise yard, Ángel pestered Dionisio Zamora for news.

"I don't know how he's doing. He was in a pretty bad way. And I'm not sure they handled it properly. Poor bastard. Heart attack. Life's a bitch."

That week. Ángel worked late every afternoon, every day.

On Sunday, when Daniel visited, Ángel told him about Salvador's heart attack. I don't know what happened, suddenly he had this pain, I told him to cough, told him it was the best thing to do. I wonder how he's doing.

On Monday the news arrived.

He pulled through, Dionisio said.

That night, Ángel heard Salvador's voice in his dream.

On Tuesday, he suddenly saw him appear in the doorway. He was pale, smiling, dressed in the same black shirt he had been wearing when they took him to the emergency room. It was only then that they worked out what had happened. The surgery had lasted several hours. Apparently, there was a doctor who was prepared to save a man's life for the fleeting, secret glory of knowing he had done so and maybe telling his family that night. But Salvador would never forget him. His name was Dr. Coronado. He had taken a section of vein from Salvador's thigh to repair the artery leading to his heart. He had toiled for hours. Salvador was fine. He would pull through. He would have to go back for regular checkups, and he would have to diet, of course. He had been told to eat half or even a third of his daily rations, barely eat at all, and exercise every day. The stir-fried beef sold at the kiosk was now forbidden fruit.

Salvador and Ángel sat and talked. They were in the main hall of the block. The air above the exercise yard glittered with a bright drizzle.

"I'm afraid to go to sleep now. I don't want that happening to me again."

"Forget it. You're fine now, compadre."

"Thing is, in hospital the nights are longer. I was used to nights here in prison, but now I know what nights are like in hospital. Nights so long, you don't know where you are. Death is always lurking somewhere nearby."

They went out into the yard, and saw some prisoners heading to the workshops. There were others gathered around the kiosk. The sky was leaden, the rain a powdery drizzle.

They pulled their jackets tighter.

"Can I tell you a story I heard in the hospital?"

"Go ahead."

"A nurse told me. She heard it from one of the nuns who goes from room to room, ministering to the sick. She said it was a woman's story, but she told me anyway."

"Yeah."

"Anyway, here goes. One day there was this patient who was dying. Dying of cancer. He was on his last legs, but still connected to a monitor, just for the sake of it. He was hardly breathing. He had that heavy labored breathing of people who are dying, struggling to find air where there's none left. He didn't need to be hooked up to machines and stuff anymore, he was near the end. No one from his family had come to see him. That night, this nun went into his room and said she was going to pray with him. So, they prayed together. The man looked up.

The nun took his hand, apparently. Sister, he said. Can I ask you a favor? Yes, my son, anything you want, the nun said. Sister, would you kiss me? What did you say, my son? Just one kiss. You have such pretty eyes. I've been dreaming about kissing you, Sister. All this time. Please, now that I'm dying, please, I want to kiss your lips. A proper kiss. Not just a peck. A kiss like they do in the movies.

"So, the nun, she glanced toward the door, looked at the patient, leaned close, and kissed him passionately, the kind of kiss that ends a movie or begins true love, the only true romance, that's how she kissed this guy as his life was draining away. Who knows who they were thinking about. Maybe they weren't thinking about anyone else. And while they were sharing that kiss, after several seconds of this passionate kiss, the guy smiled, whispered something, then sank into a deep sleep. She left him lying peacefully in his bed, shedding a tear for him, and told the ward sister she had found the man dead. I can't help but wonder, compadre, what the nun must have been thinking. It felt as though she had known this man her whole life, though she had never met him before. But she had seen him somewhere. The nun told the story to one of the nurses, but said she couldn't tell the other nurses. She had performed an act of Christian charity, she said. You tell me whether that's Christian. It's something strange, maybe beautiful, if you ask me. These are the things you learn without knowing what they mean, but there they are."

Some days later, Ángel's trial resumed, this time at the Supreme Court. He went through the various procedures to be admitted to the courtroom. It was a different prosecutor this time. Ángel felt a little nervous, but Sánchez Griñán was by his side the whole time.

On Sunday, Daniel appeared in the visitors' yard with a cheerful look on his face.

"Good news," he said to him. "Really good, this time."

"What's happened?"

The failure to carry out a gunshot residue test and the lack of witnesses worked in his favor. There wasn't a single piece of conclusive evidence against him. Sánchez Griñán had been forceful in presenting his arguments. There was not a single witness to the incident. And according to the anonymous phone call—which, though legally inadmissible, could not be ignored—a woman had seen a fat man running from the scene that night. The Supreme Court judge refused to admit this as evidence, naturally; nonetheless, he was aware that it exists. Sánchez Griñán didn't want to say anything before now so as not to get Ángel's hopes up. But, given the evidence, and the new Supreme Court judge, there was every chance of a favorable verdict. The trial would resume on Wednesday, Daniel said, and he believed Ángel would be acquitted. And I don't want to raise your hopes, but I think you'll be free by Friday.

At first, Ángel did not feel anything. It was like someone describing the sun coming out on a winter's day: something unexpected and welcome, but nothing special. But, as the day passed, he found himself feeling happier. The following morning, when he woke, he thought about the things he could do when he was released. Maybe set up a workshop where he could carry on making clay figurines, or shoes, he wasn't sure.

He spent the day talking to Salvador Ponciano.

"Fortunately, I'm staying right here," Salvador said. "I

don't know what you're going to do out there. But some-day I'll get out too, and we'll meet up."

"The thing is, I have been bored in here," Ángel said. "It's hard to stay in one place for too long."

"That's where you're wrong, compadre. All anyone is looking for in this life is a place where they can stay put. That's the thing."

That night Ángel went to sleep thinking about his room on Calle Leoncio Prado in Surquillo. He pictured the Inca Avenue arch. He knew his building was in ruins, having been flooded when the pipes burst.

His room had been the setting for so many enjoyable conversations with himself. It was where he had woken up on so many mornings. Yet during his time inside, he had forgotten about it. He preferred his bunk in the prison block. Maybe it was a throwback to his time in the barracks. But it was true. He preferred his bunk with its threadbare blanket, the bars on the windows, the work-shops, the laundry hanging in the exercise yard. Why? He looked at the photo of his mother. There are a lot of things we don't understand, but they're still in here, he said, patting his chest.

The voice answered.

Yes, a lot of things.

Yes, Mamá, he said. Yes.

He would have liked to cross that line to the other side. His mother knew it, perhaps Eliana knew it too. They knew what he was really capable of. He was there for them. Thanks to him, Eliana hadn't been charged. He was capable of staying in prison forever, of giving up the outside world, as long as Mamá and Eliana knew it. It was all that mattered to him. He was shocked by the audacity of his hope. He had wanted to be on their territory so that he could really talk to them. He had thought he would find them here, in the solitude of these months in prison.

IV

Everything went just the way he had been told it would.

On Wednesday, the judge found him not guilty. You would have been released soon anyway, your sentence was reduced because of the work you did in here, Dionisio told him.

The new prison governor, Arturo Astoray, who had cleaned up the prison and organized a routine to make the prisoners' lives more comfortable, issued the release form and the release certificate. Ángel read it, and he hugged Astoray there in his office, surrounded by the artworks given him by other inmates. The governor asked Ángel to adhere to the conditions of his release and register with one of the National Penitentiary Institute centers. But he was a free man.

He would stay one more day so that he could say goodbye to everyone. Sánchez Griñán would take care of the paperwork. The idea of his release made him happy, but he found it difficult to accept. He slept in his bunk, to the gentle sound of his cellmates' snoring. On Thursday morning, he went to the arts and crafts workshop. He had decided to make a last figurine in prison and he wanted to finish it. It was a black bull, with two white horns pointing forward, eyes staring toward the future and a gray mark in the middle of its mouth. Only a few finishing touches were needed. For a few hours, he thought only about completing it.

He was to be picked up at noon. At 11:00 a.m., he said his goodbyes to Salvador Ponciano and Dionisio Zamora.

He talked to Sinesio and to Dimas Donayre. The five of them stood chatting together for a moment in the yard. It was a Thursday in October and Father Esteban arrived to say Mass in the yard. The makeshift altar was a table, surrounded by white and purple balloons, to celebrate the Lord of Miracles.

"We are all thinking about you and praying for all of you," Father Esteban said. "You can't imagine how much."

"So, you are going back out into the world," Salvador said when the Mass was over. "I'm not sure whether to congratulate you. But don't forget to visit me, you bastard."

Ángel gave a half-smile. He had spent three years in prison. If he chose to, he could sue the State of Peru for unlawful imprisonment, but the State of Peru could file a countersuit for the food and lodging provided by taxpayers during those years. Ángel felt he should thank someone for imprisoning him, for freeing him, and for having made it possible to meet these people.

Around noon, Sánchez Griñán and his brother came to pick him up.

"Let's get out of here," he said to the photograph, slipping it into his pocket. "It's been long enough."

He felt as though his mother were asking what he planned to do. The other photo in his pocket, however, said nothing, just silently hoped he would meet the challenges of his status as a free man.

Just before he walked through the gate, he hugged Zamora again.

"That's enough now," the guard said, his eyes damp.

Ángel walked out, carrying his bag and the bull in his arms. As he squeezed past a lamppost, he miscalculated the distance, and one of the animal's legs shattered as it hit the metal bar. Ángel gripped it tightly.

"Just take it as it is. It can still stand upright."

Ángel tucked the bull under his arm.

"Marissa is waiting for us at home," Daniel said.

Ángel could hardly believe that he was looking at these crowded streets, all these people walking along, busy getting from one place to another. The street hawkers, the lampposts, the imposing buildings, it all felt like a dream suddenly materializing before his eyes. People driving cars, buses, motorcycles. All of them striving somewhat heroically to get somewhere, and adopting expressions of serene sadness as they waited in traffic jams. Just now, they inspired in him only admiration, surprise, and perhaps a little gratitude. Though none of them knew it, their faces were rekindling what you could might call his faith in life.

They walked past the Church of the Orphans, on Calle de la Chacarilla. Ángel asked his brother if they could stop for a moment. He went into the church, saw Christ with his arms outstretched, made the sign of the cross, stood for a moment in silence, and then left.

Suddenly Ángel found himself sitting in the car with his brother and the attorney. He leaned back in his seat.

"So, the case has been definitively closed?"

"Yes. Closed and filed away," said Daniel. "The authorities concluded that someone else was responsible for the murder, and it turns out that the judge had an anonymous phone call saying someone else was at the scene that night, or at least they thought so. It's not legally admissible, but it was their statement that convinced him."

Sánchez Griñán nodded as they pulled out of the parking lot.

"Do you want me to tell you something I've never told you before, Daniel?" asked the attorney.

"What?"

"I really like the center of Lima, honestly."

Daniel looked at Sánchez Griñán and smiled.

"It's a crumbling ruin, but it has a certain elegance. We keep trying to destroy it, but it's still standing. How noble it is, this city that we keep trying and failing to destroy."

The car stopped. Ángel saw a traffic cop who looked like an actor he had seen in an old movie. Then the cars began to move again.

"And what exactly do they know about the dead man?"

The attorney explained that he had been making his own inquiries.

"It turns out that the murdered man *was* Eliana's father," he said. "I looked it up in the national registry. But just recently. Her name is Eliana Cauti Espejo."

"But I thought she was an orphan. Her parents died in Ayacucho."

"I don't know the story. No one has seen her since," said Sánchez Griñán. "She must have gone off somewhere. I do know she's not living in San Juan de Miraflores anymore."

"At least she got away from him," said Daniel. "Maybe he was her father. Maybe he wasn't. One way or the other, everyone says he was an old bastard. But that doesn't matter now. Thankfully, the guy's dead and he can't harass women anymore. And you're here with us. End of story."

"I wonder where Eliana went," said Ángel.

"That's the last thing you should be thinking about, *hermano*. You and I have a lot to talk about."

Ángel said nothing. Outside the window, the pedestrians flashed past. The buses, the street vendors, the newspaper stands. Profusion and chaos, said Daniel. That's what we are. There's a little of everything, but everything is constantly moving. A rusty car plastered with stickers of the Virgin Mary pulled out in front of them. They braked sharply.

When they reached Daniel's house, Ángel found out that his brother had gotten a good price for his old Toyota station wagon. He had sold it soon after Ángel was imprisoned, and the money had been used to fund the appeal. When it had run out, Daniel had paid the attorney's fees and expenses, as well as other additional costs. Right now, the most important thing was for Ángel to find a job. Señor Alana, who owned the store in Surquillo, would not rehire him with his record. Don Paco had now retired and the store was being run by two young guys who dealt with the orders of glasses, cookware, and crockery. Don Paco had realized his dream: he had time to spend with himself. He would leaf through his newspapers, go to the cinema, listen to music, read the occasional novel. When Ángel called one day to ask him him how he was doing, Paco said: I'm poor and peaceful. I could die happy like this.

Ángel realized just how much strength his brother had given him. The help Daniel had provided was one more sign of the instinctive faith instilled in him by their mother, a strength that motivated his kindness. Daniel had visited him in prison without fail, brought the materials he needed for his work, paid off the months of back rent on his room, and, when the lease was up, collected his belongings and brought them to his own house. Ángel's clothes, washed, pressed, and ironed, had been waiting for him in a drawer in a wardrobe for the past few years.

But Ángel knew that helping him had not been the only thing on Daniel's mind. Daniel had spent these years ensuring that his transport business was thriving. He had bought new vehicles and set up local offices and parking areas for the microbuses, and was planning on starting new routes to the more distant suburbs of Lima.

"How can I ever repay you for what you've done, Daniel?"

They were in the living room of his brother's house.

Ángel glanced around him. The dark wood furniture, the cream-colored walls, and the crystal lampshade looked like trees and flowers in some paradise. Photographs of his mother and his aunts and uncles looked down on them. The floor looked spotless. Marissa had brought them glasses of beer.

"I already told you, you'll work for me. I was just taking on somebody to supervise the routes. And I need someone to change tires and fix engines. I need someone I can trust to handle the drivers' takings. That someone is you. But I'm warning you, it's a big job. I'm about to open a new office, so I'll need you there. You'll be in charge of the branch, although I'll be going back and forth to oversee things."

Ángel felt a thrill of surprise.

"Working for you . . . ? I'm not sure I'll be able . . ."

"Of course, you'll be able. You'll be working in the office."

Ángel tilted his head.

"I'm so grateful. I don't know what to say, honestly."

"Don't worry about it. For the first few months I'll pay you minimum wage, to cover what you owe me."

"Of course."

Daniel got to his feet.

"But now, let's go get some ceviche on the corner. My treat. They've started serving this amazing black clam ceviche. Do you want to come with us, Marissa?"

"You go ahead. The two of you have a lot to talk about."

As they walked to the restaurant, they reminisced about their mother. Their father's name came up, but Daniel quickly changed the subject. "I think I take after him in some ways," Ángel said. Daniel pulled a face.

"We both take after Mamá. We're nothing like him. Don't talk bullshit."

"Do you know what I learned in prison?" said Ángel, as they took their seats.

"No idea."

"That every day is its own thing. On the outside, when you're free, you don't notice it. But when you're in prison, stuck in one place, you're aware that every day is different from the last. Completely different. Because everything around you seems the same, you notice that the day is unique."

"I'm not sure I get you."

"When you're constantly looking at the same things, you see them differently every day. You notice something new in the place you were before. You look up and you see a strange cloud, you look down and there's a blade of grass growing in the yard, stuff like that. Being in prison makes you aware of things. Since you're always in the same space, it's all there is to do. You notice, I don't know, anything—a stone with white lines you hadn't seen before. Some cat that's just landed on its feet. Or a cobweb in a corner of the ceiling. It's surprising. And if you stare at something long enough, you realize that there is something miraculous about every object. Once I noticed five flowerpots on the windowsill of a nearby building. The paint on the building was peeling, it was dilapidated, but someone living there had put flowers on their windowsill. Amazing. A few flowers in the midst of nothingness, or rather in the midst of their crappy life. To me it seemed amazing, something to fucking celebrate. To be up to your neck in shit and still have the courage to put flowers on your windowsill. That was really something. Something that might save you from the nothingness. I know what I'm saying sounds crazy, it's all bullshit. But every morning I'd select some object around me as being the most beautiful. Prison forces you to pause and appreciate what you have. It forces you to imagine something beautiful, even if you don't feel like it."

They both ordered beers, tiger's milk ceviche, and black clam ceviche. They picked at the bowl of corn nuts on the table. The waiter walked away. The restaurant began to fill with young, noisy people. Young men arrived in groups, laughing and ordering rounds of beer.

"Poor bastards. . . . They're so young and they've no idea what lies in store. Look how happy they are, the dumb fucks."

Daniel smiled.

"That's the only problem with this place. Young people being loud and boisterous. But they need it to be that way."

"I'm not sure. They're a threat. Personally, I'd get rid of them. But I suppose we just have to put up with them. That's life."

The waiter arrived with the beers and the *leche de tigre*.

"Tell me something: why didn't you want to get out of that prison?"

"I did want to get out, but I also wanted to stay."

"Because you felt guilty."

Someone at the next table laughed loudly. Each of the young man's faces was frozen in a rictus of gleaming white teeth.

"I don't know. I didn't feel anything. I forgot why I was in there. There comes a point when you forget why things are the way they are. They just are, things happen and that's that. That's all there is to it. Trying to makes sense of them doesn't help. All you want is to stay where you are and stop thinking. But you can't live without thinking."

A waiter brought bottles of beer to the next table and poured them, one by one. The young men raised their glasses in a toast.

"Look at them," Daniel said.

"Yes. I wonder if we were ever like them."

"What?"

"I don't know. They laugh too much. I find it quite annoying."

The ceviche arrived. The sharp tang of the lime, the viscous salty flesh of the clams, the kernels of sweet corn, were like a revelation.

"Oh, there's something else I wanted to tell you," Daniel said.

"What?"

"Like I told you, the room you were renting is a ruin, compadre. Everything was washed away. A pipe burst and the whole building was flooded. The bed, the chairs, everything was ruined. Not that you need to worry since you were renting. But there's a room nearly ready for you in my house."

"In your house? What do you mean in your house?"

Daniel speared a piece of sweet potato with his fork. He spoke without looking up.

"You're going to come and live with us."

Ángel leaned back in his chair.

"Live in your house? Are you insane?"

"I'm not remotely insane. That's the way it's going to be."

"I can't. What will Marissa say? No. I couldn't do that. I have to find a room. I'd rather be independent, Daniel."

Daniel sipped his beer.

"Fuck being independent," he said. "It's all bull-shit. Independence—what a joke! To hell with it. Independence is something invented by young guys like them to make themselves feel better. What you need is to be with people you can talk to instead of being inside your own head all the time. You can't be alone the way you were before. You get crazy when you're alone."

"I'm not sure. But moving into your place . . . won't it bother your kids? And Marissa?"

Daniel refilled his glass with beer. Next to them, the young men were making another toast. To us, goddamn it, a voice said. To us. Another roar of laughter shook the table.

"Marissa was the one who said you should move in, compadre. She said: 'Hey, why don't you ask Ángel if he wants to live here? The kids will be thrilled too.' So shut up and drink your beer. You're going to be doing a lot of work for me, so don't argue."

Ángel savored the fibrous sweetness of the yam and held it in his mouth as long as he could. He sipped his beer.

"Okay. But . . ."

"And anyway, you're broke, remember? All you own are the clothes you've got on you right now. And with a criminal record, there aren't many people who will offer you work. And you're a bit old to go back to wrestling."

"I know. Though you don't need to go on about it."

"The money you gave me from the sale of the figurines went to the attorney and the court fees. I had to consult a lot of people. And I also had to put some money toward them."

They sat in silence. Ángel was relieved by this turn in the conversation. He owed his brother a great deal, but he knew he would get the chance to pay him back. He began to eat the corn kernels one by one. The taste brought him back to the world and he felt a strange flash of joy.

"I don't know how to thank you."

"Don't worry."

Ángel took a huge mouthful.

"Look, have it your way," he conceded. "If you like, I'll work for you in the office. Actually, I probably know the routes. Since I did deliveries, I know a lot of barrios. I know the streets. But you have to listen when I give advice."

"Sure. I'll always take your advice. So, that's it, it's settled. Consider it done, compadre."

They ate for a while in silence. Then they started to talk about work. The performance of the engines needed to be improved, the oil needed to be checked regularly. For an engine to last, it was important to change the oil regularly, Daniel told him.

"Tell me something, Daniel."

"What?"

"Do you know anything else about Eliana?"

His brother drained his beer and pressed a napkin to his lips.

"Nothing. And I've no reason to find out. What I know, I told you in the car. I don't think we will be hearing about her ever again."

The waiter came over with the dessert menu. Ángel wasn't sure if he wanted a *suspiro de limeña* or some *picarones*.

"Let's get both," Daniel said.

They spent the rest of the lunch talking about going to Mass on Sunday with their mother and having lunch in places like this. After a while, the waiter brought the bill.

"Do you remember when we lived up in Ayacucho?"

"Of course. But that was more than forty years ago. What's the point in remembering?"

"You're right."

The two men walked to the door. They left behind the young men's clamor and were engulfed by the bustle of the street outside.

That afternoon Ángel went to buy clothes at a department store and emerged with a bag containing two pairs of pants, five shirts, underwear, socks, and a box containing a pair of black shoes that were a little tight but would do. Then he went to the bank and deposited what little money was left from the sale of his figurines. Finally, he bought a new cell phone. He looked at the device as though it were an extension of himself. Now you will become somebody. You're not a person, you're a phone number, Daniel had said.

He felt exhausted. His shoulders ached. He went for a stroll around his brother's neighborhood. Coming to a park, he sat down on a low wall and watched the trees swaying in the breeze.

By the time he got back to Daniel's house, it was dark. His niece and nephew, Vanessa and Jorge, were doing homework in the dining room. Ángel remembered some of the algebra problems—his favorite subject—and managed to solve the model equations that Vanessa was studying for a test the following day.

Then he poured himself a glass of beer, sat down to watch the news, and, after a while, realized he had not yet been in the room that was to be his, at least for a time.

"Right, your room is all ready," Marissa said suddenly.

He followed her to the end of a corridor. She opened a door and Ángel saw something he could never have imagined.

"See you tomorrow, Ángel," Marissa said. "Sleep well."

Ángel found himself alone. The bed was neatly made up, clean sheets and orange blankets on a mattress supported by a polished wooden base. On the bedside table was a glowing lamp, a small pile of books, and a plastic box with a brush, some toothpaste, towels, soap, and bottles of shampoo and conditioner. Marissa had arranged things to create a welcoming place.

Ángel sat looking at the brush, the long bristles reaching out as though to help him, to protect him, to keep him in the world. The brush was round and nestled comfortably in his hand and, at that moment, the blue and white pattern was the gentlest thing he had ever seen. Around him lay the soap, the towels, the neatly made bed. As he gazed at these tangible objects placed there for him, he felt his head explode, watched as reality blurred, reordered itself and confirmed what, until now, he had not fully believed: somebody was welcoming him back into the world. He spent a time he could not measure lost in a dizzying whirl. In the darkness, he saw many of the images that had been hounding him, felt the overwhelming solace of tears, and sank into the air around him. Eventually, sobbing, he realized that he was still there on his bed.

The following morning, after breakfast, Daniel said goodbye to his brother.

"I'll see you at the office."

"I'll be there in a little while."

"Where are you going?"

"To see someone."

Ángel arrived at the hospital entrance and walked over to the reception desk.

"Captain Nicolás?" he asked.

The duty nurse checked her monitor, then turned to him.

"The captain died last week," she said. "I'm so sorry. Are you a member of the family?"

"No."

Ángel stood in silence.

"Did someone arrange for the body to be collected?"

The nurse took out a notebook. She was writing something.

"Yes. It says here that a woman took him," she said without looking at him.

"A relative?"

The nurse shrugged. She closed the notebook and placed it in a drawer.

"I don't know. I'd have to check his records."

Just then, her phone rang and she answered. She glanced up and down the corridor now and then as she spoke. She was saying something about visiting her mother that night. After a moment, she hung up.

"There is a visitors' book," the nurse said. "For those who want to sign it."

Ángel took the book from her, signed his name, and drew a skull and crossbones.

So, you've abandoned me now, Captain, he said to himself as he got out of a taxi and walked slowly past the line of traffic.

His thoughts melded with the thud of his footsteps and the roar of engines. I guess you figured your mission was accomplished. But I came to tell you something. Your mission was not accomplished, Captain. But I'm not interested in it anymore. You've gone AWOL, and I won't ever think about you again. I don't even want to know where you're buried, what d'you think about that? Better for me. Goodbye forever, Captain. Patting his chest, Ángel added: And I hope you never rest in peace, because you'll always be in here.

Shortly afterward, Ángel arrived at Transportes Serpa in the Ate neighborhood. The offices had been expanded while he was in prison. Behind the security gate and the varnished wood door was a large room filled with

Formica tables. There were desks, chairs, and a map of the city with routes marked out by long arrows. A polished glass door led out to a yard where microbuses were parked like horses in a stable. There was a workshop, with a wheel repair lathe and water tanks, and a stud wall with a door that led to a toilet. At the back was a storage area for buckets, rags, and brooms.

In one office, two men were sitting at computers. In the other, Daniel greeted Señora Norma, his secretary, then sat at his desk and introduced "my brother Ángel." Then he introduced the drivers and mechanics: Donato, Pocho, and Beto.

"That's the team. The guys with the flabby asses spend all day driving, the other guys spend all day sitting on their asses at desks. One way or another, everybody here works their ass off. If they didn't, nothing would work."

"Good to meet you," Ángel said.

The men smiled at him, then looked to their boss.

"Tell everyone there's a meeting in the yard in ten minutes," Daniel told Señora Norma.

Within minutes, twenty drivers were gathered in the yard. Daniel went to speak to them. I just wanted to say again how much I appreciate your hard work, he began. We're getting more and more passengers. And I also wanted to give you some good news. I have secured a bank loan to buy new tires for the entire fleet. I have also contracted with a garage to routinely fine-tune the engines and touch up the bodywork. As soon as possible, a repair shop will be set up next door, on this same street, to make work easier. Things are going to get better. That's a promise.

Then he nodded to Ángel. This is my brother Ángel

Serpa. He'll be working for the company from now on, handling routing and maintenance. He'll be here to deal with any queries, to help with repairs and maintenance and supervise the ticket books. From now on, I'll be spending less time here because we're opening a new branch in Los Olivos. I appreciate your cooperation. I'll still pop by now and then. A big thanks to all of you, I'll see you soon.

The drivers drifted away. When he was alone with Ángel in his office, Daniel said:

"The first thing you need to do is ensure people respect you and feel you appreciate their work. But you also need to make sure they see you as a leader. We need to improve the fleet, that's the aim. You can use the money budgeted as 'miscellaneous' for whatever you might need. This place is all yours now, compadre."

Ángel spent that evening out in the parking lot. He inspected every bus and made a checklist. The seats needed to be reupholstered, that was the first thing. Passengers should be able to remember their vehicles by their look. All the vehicles needed to be painted in the same livery so they stood out. Tires and shock absorbers were quickly worn down through use and needed to be constantly checked.

The following day, Ángel visited a series of tire shops looking for the best deal. That evening he suggested to Daniel that they play music on the buses—salsa, reggaetón, waltzes, even *boleros*, why not. Their microbuses had wider seats than their competitors, something passengers appreciated. But customers don't see our business as *different*. All right, Daniel agreed. Let's give it a go. And you can use some of the profits to repaint the fleet.

One night when he got home, he found his nephew, Jorge, at the table in the dining room, typing something into his laptop with a worried look on his face.

"Hey, uncle."

"Hey, Jorge, something wrong?"

"No, I'm fine. Just thinking."

"About what?"

"I don't know what to do," he said.

"About what?"

"Kids at school say you were in prison. That you're a murderer and now you're living here with us. Is that true?"

Ángel sat down next to him.

"No, it's not true, Jorge. I don't know exactly what they've said. But it's not true."

"So, what did happen?"

"Listen, it was all a bit of a blur. A guy on the street was threatening me. And then someone showed up out of nowhere and shot the guy threatening me. Since I was there, they blamed me. But I didn't do it. Honestly, I didn't."

"I get it, *tío*."

Ángel leaned closer.

"The proof is that I was released. Listen: they had no evidence. Nothing. The truth is, the reason I stayed in prison for so long was because I wanted to."

"All right."

"But I learned a few things inside."

Jorge looked at him.

"Like what?"

"How to make my ceramic figurines. Have you seen the bull in my bedroom? It had four legs when I got out, but one of them broke. I knocked it against a lamppost. Now it's only got three. But it can still stand up straight."

Jorge was looking at him.

"So, how are you really doing?" Ángel asked his nephew.

"I'm fine. But I've just realized something. Something that never occurred to me."

"What?"

"Okay, I'll tell you, but I don't want anyone else to know. Especially not Papá."

"Tell me."

"There's this girl. I can't stop thinking about her."

Ángel smiled.

"Is she in your class?"

"She's in fourth grade, a year below. But I see her during recess. And today I went over to her. I went right up to her."

"And?"

"I said it was a nice day. She was with her girlfriends. And I gave her a chocolate bar. I'd bought the chocolate specially for her."

"And how did she react?"

"Fine. I think it was fine. We chatted for a bit. It was the first time we've ever talked. She's so pretty, *tío*. You should see her."

"That's great. And does she like you?"

"I don't know. What can I do to make her like me? Her name's Paula."

"I don't know. Give her little gifts. Give her something. Talk to her about school stuff. You probably have some of the same teachers . . ."

"She has the teachers I had last year."

"Well, talk about them. About their work. About

homework, anything. Make her laugh, if you can. Tell her
a joke. That always works."

"Okay. I'll try."

"Go up to her tomorrow at recess. Bring her some
cookies."

"Do you think she'd like that?"

"Look. Here's some money to buy them."

Ángel took out some coins.

"Okay. Thanks, *tío*."

Ángel went to his room. It never would have occurred
to him that he would be good at giving romantic advice,
but he realized that he enjoyed it. It almost made him
feel happy.

He went back to the prison several times over the following Sundays to visit his friends and tell them what he was
up to. It felt normal, having to pass through security to
get to the exercise yard. After all, one way or another, he
had always been a suspect. Once he had been searched,
he was given a metal token, and that made him feel
reassured.

The first time he went, he talked to Salvador Ponciano.
I'm feeling pretty good because they're reviewing my
case, Salvador said. They say there are mitigating circumstances, so I might even be released, can you imagine? It's possible that my wife is going to retract her
statement. I'm sure my daughter put her up to it. So, she
might retract, although she'd better not expect me to be
grateful. Anyway, I've served almost half my sentence
now. It's strange, what with one thing and another, the
years rolled by.

A week later, they told Ángel that Dimas Donayre had
been released and had gone back to his family in Cusco.

Of his friends in prison, only Sinesio and Salvador were still behind bars. For a time, Ángel visited every weekend. Some Sundays, Dionisio Zamora would be in the exercise yard.

"You haven't changed a bit," Dionisio said, hugging Ángel. "And neither have I."

On the morning that the company's new buses went into operation, Ángel stood by inside the garage gates. From there he could see the buses in their newly painted livery driving down the street. It was a moment of glory.

The following day, he suggested to Daniel that they could ask a priest to bless the fleet. Ángel tried to contact Father Esteban, but Dionisio Zamora said no one had heard from him. Father Vincent, the new prison chaplain, came and blessed the buses. Some of the drivers listened with heads bowed. One asked whether they could put an image of Sarita Colonia, "The People's Saint," in their buses, and the priest agreed, as long as the saint and her followers revered the Lord.

From their first day out, the new microbuses added more passengers. Drivers came back to the garage early with their ticket books almost empty. After a few months, Daniel purchased two more vehicles, then another two. They would need to build a bigger garage or sell off a few of the older buses.

More than two months had passed since Ángel's release and he had been considering what he should do.

He spent a whole weekend thinking about it, and on Monday, phoned up to say he would be coming in late. This was as good a day as any for what he had planned.

He went out and hailed a taxi. He did not find it odd

that the car that pulled up was a station wagon exactly like the one he had driven, or that the driver looked a little like him. He told him he was going to Calle Alipio Ponce, and the man seemed to nod as though he had known he would be taking him there.

It was ten o'clock when he arrived. He paid the driver, got out of the taxi, and stood in front of the house.

He stared at the black railings. The paint was peeling, and not one of the blue geraniums that used to grow on the windowsill remained. Outside the bodega on the corner was a sign placed by the local council that said "CLOSED." Some of the houses had been recently repainted. In every other way, the street where Eliana used to live (or still lived?) looked exactly as it had some years earlier.

Ángel walked up to the door, paused, and glanced back at the street. There was no one around. It was as though all the neighbors had conspired to ensure he would be alone.

He rang the doorbell. A breeze stirred the branches next to him. A car horn honked. He rang again.

Then he heard a voice. Who's there? He did not know what to say. I'm looking for Eliana, he said. Who is it? said the voice. Eliana. Señorita Eliana Cauti. She lives here, doesn't she?

A wrinkled old woman appeared. A few stray curls fell over her forehead, her eyes were deep-set and distant. She spoke with a drawl.

"Who are you looking for?" she asked.

Her eyes suddenly flared into life. Staring through the screen door, they were the eyes of a mole in its burrow that has scented something potentially interesting.

"I'm looking for Eliana Cauti. She used to live here."

"I don't know any Eliana. And I've been living here for a year, Señor."

Ángel stepped closer.

"You didn't know the previous owners?"

"No. There's nobody here. I live alone. I don't have anything, Señor."

"I didn't mean to bother you. I'm just looking for Eliana. She used to live here."

The woman seemed to be thinking.

"The previous owners left a long time ago. My son bought this house for me."

"And he doesn't know anything about them?"

The woman peered at him with her sunken eyes. Something seemed to occur to her. She was silent for a moment.

"Just a minute. Wait there."

She closed the door. After a moment, she reappeared with a piece of paper.

"They left this address."

Ángel took out a pen and a notebook and jotted down the address. It was on Calle Pérez Roca in Barranco.

The woman retrieved the piece of paper.

"Thank you," Ángel said as she shut the door.

In a way, he felt relieved. He had done his duty and tried to track her down. But he had had no idea what he would say if he had found her. Thinking about it, he realized he had simply wanted to see her, to make sure that she knew he was all right. He did not know why, but he thought perhaps Eliana had been worrying about him all this time.

He went back out to the street and walked to the corner. He would have to walk a couple of blocks before he could hail a taxi.

Suddenly he stopped. The house Eliana's father had come from was right in front of him. The same dark bricks, the long railing, the aluminum window frames. But there was something new. A large sign. FOR SALE.

Ángel stopped and looked at the house. There were cracks in the walls and something strange and sinister about the door: one of the panels was splintered and was marked with damp stains. He went closer. This was the house Huarón had emerged from on the night he died.

As he approached the door, he realized it was just a few wooden planks held closed by a piece of wire. If he could bend the wire, he could get into the house. He gripped it with his fingers and twisted. Eventually, the wire begin to give way and the door moved. He twisted again. He found himself standing inside a ruined house.

The cracked floor was covered with dust and stones and the remnants of some wooden beams. At the back, he found a ruined brick wall, shattered windows, and a huge water tank. He seemed to be breathing nothing but dust.

Ángel suddenly felt as though the place was familiar. He gingerly stepped over the piles of dust and stones. There was a new silence, something he had not noticed when he first came in.

He approached a door, the largest door. Maybe it led to a bedroom. He felt scared. What was he doing there? He wanted to know who that man had been. Had he really been Eliana's father? Was what his brother had told him true?

He reached out and turned the handle. The door slowly opened. He stepped into a large room with gold wallpaper and black-and-white floor tiles that were worn from use. On one wall, a mirror hung at an angle.

Unexpectedly, something moved. There was an old man in the corner. He was wearing a striped shirt, grimy pants, and cracked shoes and was sitting cross-legged on a crumpled sofa, swinging one foot from side to side. He peered curiously at Ángel. He smiled, a long, malicious smile.

Then his eyes flickered. They settled on some fixed point in the distance.

Ángel walked slowly toward him. The man's mouth now hung open in a frozen rictus. His disheveled white hair pointed in every direction. Suddenly he turned his huge, deep-set eyes on Ángel. Stared at him like an animal gazing into the distance, befuddled by something unfamiliar.

It dawned on Ángel that someone had shut the man up in here and would probably come back soon to feed him or take him somewhere else. Somebody who did not want to look after the old man but would come from time to time and bring him a few crusts.

Ángel had once read an article in a newspaper about elderly people abandoned in derelict houses. Sick, destitute people forced to live alone. People who never go outside. Sometimes, a relative would bring them food, but not often. It happens because families don't want to take them in and cannot afford to put them in a nursing home. So they abandon them, leave them in some run-down house because they don't know what else to do.

Ángel was still standing in front of the man. Still looking at his face with its patchy white beard. Something moved. The man smiled again. It was a cruel smile. The smile of someone who recognized Ángel after a long time. There was a piercing iciness in the man's eyes, as though he knew and understood everything Ángel had been through. There came a sound from outside on the street. Abruptly, the man's features shifted and he returned to his former stupor. He gazed at nothing in particular, his eyes fixed on the empty air.

For a moment, Ángel considered getting him something to eat or drink. Was this man one of Huarón's relatives? Why was he here if the house was up for sale?

He felt his cell phone vibrate against his body. Ángel started. He took a step back. He left the room.

It was his nephew Jorge.

"Hey, *tío*."

Ángel went outside. He could barely keep hold of the phone.

"Hey, Jorge."

"I wanted to ask your advice about something."

"I'm on my way home. I'll be there soon."

When he reached the sidewalk, he broke into a run. He glanced behind. The wind stung his eyes. He ran faster and faster.

Eventually, he reached the avenue but even then he did not stop. He had to keep going. He ran along the verge as a line of cars hurtled past.

He stopped and bent over, resting his hands on his knees. He was gasping for breath.

He spotted a black car with a checkered yellow-and-white stripe. He raised a hand.

"Taxi?" said the young man behind the wheel.

Ángel clambered in.

He was still clutching the address in Barranco. The address where Eliana was supposedly living now.

"Take me to Calle Pérez Roca," he said.

When he reached the street, he started his search. The

number he had written down was 247. He passed several houses. 241, 245, and 249. The next house was 253. Perhaps he had misread the seven and it was actually 241. He stopped in front of that door. Knocked once. No answer. He knocked twice more. Was this really where Eliana was living? Suddenly, he was overcome by a wave of exhaustion. He took two steps backward. He saw a group of schoolchildren on the corner. They were probably playing hooky from school.

Ángel wandered away from the house, heading toward the traffic circle on the seafront. He walked past a store called Dédalo and looked at people standing meditatively in the garden. When he reached the seafront, he sat down. Above him hung a bougainvillea that swayed from side to side. A breeze caressed his face. Before him, the sea stretched away in shades of steel and gray, streaked with flashes of white.

Why should he continue with this search? What was it that he wanted to say to Eliana? Would he be able to really speak to her?

He sat for a while, staring out at the horizon. To his left, the headland of Morro Solar seemed to proudly rise up from the waters. He had never looked at it this way before.

He decided to move on. He strolled along the leafy central island running down the middle of the Avenida Saenz Peña. He passed glass doors set into wooden façades. He came again to the house that might have been Eliana's. Leaving it behind, he walked as far as the corner, where he hailed a taxi.

He had to get to work, but first he would stop by the house. After all, his nephew wanted to ask him for advice.

"So, what's up, Jorge?" he asked.

"Hey, *tío*. I didn't go to school today."

"Why not?"

"We had a math test and I don't know anything. But they're going to make me take it tomorrow. Can you help me? It's on linear equations and I can't figure them out at all. Then we'll probably have to do nonlinear equations."

Within six months of starting work, Ángel had made himself indispensable. He woke at dawn every day and was always first through the door, just ahead of Señora Norma, who would make him his first coffee.

One day, he decided they should build a shrine to the Virgen de las Nieves next to the parking lot. He commissioned two craftsmen, who worked on if for a week. When they had finished, Ángel stood for a long moment before the image of the Virgin Mary, gazing heavenward. Occasionally, when he passed it, Ángel would mutter a prayer under his breath, and that calmed him.

He also decided to set up a stall selling juice, sodas, sandwiches, and empanadas. He considered asking Tania or Señora Adelaida from Surquillo market to man the stall, but thought they were probably busy doing other things. In the end, he gave the job to the daughter of one of the drivers, something for which the man was very grateful.

Shortly afterward, Ángel appointed himself head of the cleaning detail. His first course of action was to hire an energetic group of boys who would show up with brooms, buckets, and sponges. Sometimes, Ángel would help out himself. When he finished the day's work, he would take the photo of his mother from his pocket, give her an account of his day and listen to what she had to say.

Everything with the drivers was going well, with a few rare exceptions. Now and again, a notice about a traffic fine would arrive. The company would pay the fine and deduct the money from the driver's salary. During this period, a few drivers had to be let go for accidents that occurred while they were speeding. Others had been caught drinking in the office after hours.

Daniel decided to introduce a system whereby a driver was paid a salary and an additional bonus based on the passenger numbers on each trip. However, there would be deductions for any accidents or complaints, he warned.

Ángel and Daniel realized that the success of the business depended on two factors that, though straightforward, were nonetheless difficult to accomplish: keeping the microbuses properly maintained, and keeping the minds, bodies, and hearts of the drivers and fare collectors fully operational. If these could both be achieved, the company would be better equipped to take on the unrelenting madness of Lima traffic. Over time, his brother entrusted Ángel with a new responsibility: interviewing applicants for driver vacancies.

To do this, Ángel had a desk installed by the front door. An applicant would hand over their documentation and then Ángel would ask questions, looking him straight in the eye. It was the same method he had adopted as a salesman, whenever a new customer walked in. Look them in the eye, note the shape of their face, the tone of their voice. There were no hard-and-fast rules for these evaluations, only an impression given off by the faces of the applicants. The symmetry of a candidate's features, the color of his eyes, the firmness of his tone were indicative of his private morality. Sometimes the shape of a man's mouth mattered more than his references. "You can tell from the shape of someone's lips whether he's spent his whole life telling lies," he told Daniel. "Liars' lips are thinner because they purse them so much."

One morning, as he was sweeping the yard, he took the photo of the captain from his pocket and dropped it in the trash.

That same morning, when he went back to his desk, he decided he needed to get away from the office. It was time to go and search for a better deal on tires; he could visit a few dealers along the Avenida Tomás Marsano.

He checked out several tire stores. One had an offer on radial tires for microbuses.

After examining them, he decided to go to Surquillo market for lunch, the way he used to.

In the market, next to the expressway, by the soaring wall of billboards and powerlines, Tania was surprised to see him.

"Señor Ángel."

"I came for lunch. Just like old times, Tania."

"When did you get out of prison, Señor Ángel?"

"A few months ago. I've been meaning to come here for a while."

"So, what will it be? A *patasca*?"

"Maybe *causa de cangrejo*, Tania. I always wanted to try something like that."

"I'll bring it right over."

Then Ángel noticed a little boy. He was about two or three years old and he was standing next to Tania. He stared at Ángel with his huge eyes.

"That's Miguel," she said. "He's helping me already."

Ángel shook the child's hand. He wished the boy was his.

"A handsome little boy," he said, "So cute."

He lingered over lunch until late. He needed to go back to the office. He could place the order for the tires on his way.

That night, his niece Vanessa was waiting for him with a question.

"*Tío*, tell me, did you used to be a wrestler?"

"Yes, Vane."

"Could you take me to see a fight? I'd love to go."

"Absolutely not," said a voice from the dining room. It was Marissa.

"I'll take you, don't worry, but you might have to wait a couple of years," Ángel said.

Vanessa pulled a face.

"Do you promise to take me as soon as I turn eighteen?"

That Friday, Ángel decided to go to the fights at Cancha de los Muertos in Chorrillos. He caught a cab and arrived at 9:30 p.m., his usual time. As he walked toward the tent, the roar gradually grew louder. The path up the hill had not changed, and he arrived with his shoes covered in dust. He paid the entry fee and spotted El Gordo.

"What brings you here?"

"I came to see how you're doing."

"We're screwed, worse than before. The wrestlers are getting old and most of them have gone somewhere else. We've only got a few left. People still come to watch. But no one fights to kill anymore. No one gets hurt. I don't even have a medic anymore. They wrestle just to pass the time. And for the money. It isn't what it used to be."

"What can you do, people get more civilized and the whole world goes to hell. Times change."

El Gordo grinned.

"Hey, why don't you get changed and fight tonight? I have a wrestler for you."

"Thanks, but no thanks, amigo," Ángel said, raising his hands. "I've retired."

"That's a bitch. Well, take a seat. Scorpion Gómez is about to fight. You should see the guy."

"Scorpion Gómez?"

"Yeah, he got the name from some story or other. He'll be out any minute."

Ángel sat in the bleachers. Soon afterward, more spectators started to trickle in. They were not the monsters he was used to from the time when he fought here. They lacked the tattoos, the scars, the gravelly voices for shouting insults. They were thin and soft-spoken. They lined up to place their bets and then went back to their seats.

Ángel watched Scorpion Gómez strut out. He was a tall guy with long arms and a nose like an iron hook. That night he was wrestling Taita Mena, someone Ángel knew. Taita's hair was streaked with gray these days, and his face was distorted by deep wrinkles.

The fight did not last long. Scorpion wrapped his arms around Taita and squeezed all the air out of him. Taita's face swelled and turned purple, as though it might explode. When Scorpion let him drop, Taita stayed on the canvas. El Gordo had to intervene to stop Scorpion from kicking him in the chest.

The strangest thing was that when Taita finally got to his feet, he went over and hugged Scorpion before walking off. El Zapallo Reina and El Cabo Gutarra, Ángel's old acquaintances, came out to clean the fight cage.

Two new brawlers stepped into the ring. Ángel barely gave them a glance.

He got up and walked out into a drizzle. He looked up the hill. A net of clouds was advancing, like a herd of docile animals returning to the past.

V

One Monday, a tall, slim young woman with legs like a gazelle walked into the office. She brought a folder containing several references and a resume. She was applying for an administrative vacancy. She climbed the steps warily and paused, looking around for someone to speak to. Her blue suit, black shoes, disciplined hands, and long, flowing hair were all indicative of someone who had surmounted a wall of insecurities to venture out into the world. Her eyes flickered from side to side with unhurried concern. Ángel was spellbound by her slender neck. He suddenly imagined someone appearing behind her to try and slit her throat. He felt he needed to be there to prevent such a thing from happening.

"Her name is Julia," he told the photograph of his mother that evening. "I don't know what I'm going to do."

Shortly afterward, he heard his mother's response.

The following Monday, Julia was working at the desk next to his. Ángel gave her some directions about the routes and the supervision of the vehicles, and she picked them up instantly.

On her first few days, she and Ángel arrived at the office at the same time. They oversaw the departure of the first buses, distributed ticket books to the drivers, and checked that the brakes on the buses were working. On days when Ángel arrived a little later, Julia would tell him about any incidents and he would take care of them.

Julia came to work wearing white or blue blouses and

black cotton trousers. She wore low-heeled shoes that revealed her slender feet. Her long, liquid eyes always seemed to be giving him a sidelong glance. Before long, they were telling each other about their lives. One afternoon, while writing something, he told her that he had been in prison, after being charged with a crime he did not commit. She told him that the judiciary and the police routinely made mistakes, but that did not mean we should resign ourselves to living in such a world. This, she told him, was what she had been taught both at home and at school. She had attended the parish school in Lince, and was the only child of rather elderly parents. But neither had prepared her for the struggle against evil in the world, she confessed. So, we must learn to face our problems alone as best we can. But that was as it should be, she added with a smile. Until now she had been working as a schoolteacher, but she loved working in the office with him.

After a month of seeing her every day and dreaming about her every night, Ángel made up his mind. One afternoon, as they were going through the piles of paperwork on their desks, he plucked up the courage to ask:

"Would you like to go for a drink, just here on the corner?"

She was picking up a document. One hand hovered over the desk.

"I'd love to. Let me just finish up with these and we can go," she said.

They spent the evening chatting in the restaurant on the corner. At first, they ordered only water and crackers. Later they ordered two beers. For a while she had thought about being a *bolero* singer, she said. "But I realized I was much happier singing alone in my room. It's something I should probably be embarrassed by, but it cheers me up," she whispered with a smile.

In the days that followed, Ángel caught himself staring at her, sitting in front of her screen, her blouse pale, her complexion radiant. A stray lock of hair fell against her taut neck.

One afternoon, they stayed chatting in the office long after everyone had gone home. When they finally left, he hailed a cab for her.

"Why don't we go see a movie?" Ángel said. "Tonight, I mean. What do you think?"

"I'd need to go home to get ready," she said with a smile, as she toyed with her hair.

When he arrived at her house by the Plaza de Lince a few hours later, Julia was wearing a cream dress. Her hair looked silken, her skin luminous, and on her eyes was a subtle trace of blue eyeshadow. She introduced Ángel to her parents. Her father wore a striped flannel shirt, and his neat hair was thinning. Her mother wore a blouse with ribbons. They got to their feet to shake hands with him.

After the movie, Ángel and Julia walked to a Chinese restaurant on the corner. They sat at a large table, next to an air conditioner. They shared a plate of crispy noodles and pickled radishes. They praised the texture of the meat in black bean sauce. They decided to order a beer, and then another. As the evening went on, they found new things to talk about. I love music, Julia said, but I like the kind of music no one else does. *Boleros*, waltzes, some *baladas*. Her smile lit up her face. Ángel quivered at the sight of the smooth, pale skin of her shoulders. From this still point on her body, the whole world seemed to set itself in motion.

Ángel got back to his room around midnight, but he did not fall asleep for a long time.

On Monday morning, at the office, they carried on chatting as the drivers arrived. The new routes we've set up are going from strength to strength, he told her. I think it's down to the fact that the drivers are decent guys; in a sense, they're our heroes, though no one realizes it. They're heroes, I really believe that. The drivers. The fare collectors. It's amazing that they haven't been driven mad by the traffic. Luckily, most of them are religious and they have their patron saints. Of all the Virgin Marys, the most popular among the drivers is Our Lady of Otuzco, La Virgen de la Puerta. But there are others too. People feel a lot calmer riding with them, they feel as though God and the Virgin Mary are by their side. That's always reassuring.

When Julia talked, her hands reached downward, as though organizing space. Every phrase, spoken with melodious lightness, seemed to imbue reality with a gentle symmetry. It was as though she had spent a long time practicing to be with him. And he could only feel grateful for the studied naturalness of her presence. The world had been whirling, only to stop in this precise instant.

When he woke in the morning, Ángel longed only to hear her voice. As he drifted off to sleep, he pictured her slender arms, the gold bracelet around her wrist, the perfect curves of her white nails. One morning, seeing himself in the mirror, he realized his face had recovered its composure. A little later, over breakfast, he told Daniel that when he was with Julia it felt as though his bones returned to their rightful places.

One Friday, after work, they took a microbus and

drove around Kennedy Park in Miraflores. They ate in a Middle Eastern restaurant and walked as far as the seafront. They sat, gazing at the lights, at the streaks of white borne aloft by the wind. They stared into the darkness dotted with lights, talking and slipping into shared silences.

During a lull in the conversation, Ángel leaned close and kissed Julia for what seemed like an eternity. He felt the moist firmness of her parting lips, the pale quiver of her skin, the long, smooth surfaces of her arms around his neck. They sat locked in their embrace. They were at one with the sky unfurling above, ringed by the lights of the Bay of Lima. After a while, as though responding to a mutual impulse, they got up and strolled until they reached a hotel on Calle Grau.

The staircase was narrow; the room had orange curtains and small bedside lamps that took some time to warm up.

They threw themselves on the bed and kissed. He peeled off his shirt. Julia tried to take off her sweater, but for some reason, she couldn't. It clung to her body and the woolen neck seemed too small for her head to pass through. She opened her purse and pointed to something; Ángel found a pair of scissors among the various objects.

"Cut it off," she said.

Ángel hesitated, but she nodded.

He began cutting away her sweater, little by little, until he saw a red blouse with white buttons, then her neck, her breasts, and her upraised arms.

That night, for the first time in a long time, Ángel felt the warm force of a woman. She had come from a place he had always imagined as his own. Julia's firm skin compelled him to rise to the challenge. He trembled as he touched her breasts. Fear was a part of love. The fear of losing her, of not being worthy, of simultaneously longing to be someone else and to be himself. His body constantly made him aware of the needs that until now it had suppressed, the need to feel safe, to feel appreciated, to be acknowledged by another person. He felt the moisture of a sadness that had just been released, the vertigo of skin brushing against his own. He shuddered as he discovered Julia. He felt naked, exposed to all the things she had intuited but had not said. Never had he imagined the white heat of the light in that hotel room. It was the secret glow that Julia had managed to discern within his body, the one that, from now on, he knew would sustain him. He felt so ecstatic and so serene, felt a tiredness that was as welcome as it was unexpected, and after making love several times he fell asleep on her shoulder.

From that night, they always returned to the same room. Julia offered him a boundless universe of sensation, one that expanded those things he had felt when he saw her appear in his office that first afternoon, in her blue suit and her black shoes, her voice drifting in. Watching her undress, entering her, immersing himself forever in the gentle firmness of her body, these were gifts he felt he did not deserve and could not explain. Julia had become a home to him. One day, she told him that all she wanted was for him to be happy and at peace. It was astounding. They made love as though performing a ritual of purification, freeing themselves of the dregs of his suffering, each of them trying to reach the farthest reaches of the other's imagination.

For the first time in a long time, Ángel felt the urge to wander the streets, even if only to stroll around the neighborhood. He no longer spent his weekends at home or in the office. He spent them with her, sometimes with her parents and friends, but he was happiest when it was just the two of them. They went window-shopping, went to the cinema, began to meet new people in her neighborhood. Sometimes Ángel would stop and gaze at passersby and their faces seemed wonderful for some reason. In restaurants, the dishes he was served tasted of something. He began to work harder and more joyfully. He made friends with some of the drivers, and they introduced him to their wives. Sometimes Julia would come and eat at Daniel's house, with Marissa, Jorge, and Vanessa.

Twice, Julia accompanied him to the prison, although Sinesio was no longer there. Dionisio Zamora had also decided to retire. One of his daughters had just come back from the United States and he decided to go and live with her. Only Salvador Ponciano remained, "but I'll be out of here soon, compadre, it's only a matter of weeks now." Ángel once again explained to his girlfriend how he had been imprisoned here after being falsely charged with murder. He had seen the murderer flee the scene. He had gotten out of his car and had been standing, resting on a corner. It was then that he had found the body, and the gun lying on the ground. That was his story. But fortunately, with the help of his brother and a good attorney, the matter had been cleared up. Even so, he had spent three years in prison. Every time he raised the subject, Julia would lay a hand against his cheek.

One Monday, over breakfast with Daniel, Ángel announced that he was going to move into an apartment.

He would apply for a bank loan and buy a place, maybe somewhere near the office.

"That's fine, *hermano*. I've been expecting this for a while now," Daniel said. "Besides, the business is growing, and the family is too."

Ángel married Julia in the early days of a warm December, at the church of Santa Beatriz de Lince. Father Vincent officiated. Almost two years had passed since Ángel had been released from prison.

On the day of the ceremony, Ángel wore a dark suit and declined the white boutonniere his father-in-law offered with a smile. It's not my style. Flowers in my lapel don't suit me (and I'm no Knight of the Roses either, he thought to himself).

Julia wore a rustic ivory silk dress trimmed with tulle. That morning she had put on a little makeup. Ángel and her friends agreed that she had never looked more beautiful.

The ceremony was attended by a great many family members, especially on Julia's side. But Daniel, Marissa, Jorge, and Vanessa were also there in the front row. In the rear pews, Ángel's friends were bathed in gentle sunlight. As the couple emerged after taking their vows, Dimas Donayre, Sinesio, and Salvador Ponciano, who had just been released, were among the people waiting in line to congratulate them. Next to Salvador was a young woman in a green dress with almond eyes and pointed ears. Her name was Yesenia and she walked through life hanging on her boyfriend's arm with a smile and a promise she had made herself: she would never leave him.

"Let me introduce you to my fiancé," Salvador announced, nodding to her. "Or better still, this is my enchantress."

Next to him, Yesenia smiled and kissed them with her red-stained lips. "A pleasure to meet you," she trilled in a birdlike voice, offering her cheek to anyone who approached.

Dionisio Zamora also came to the ceremony. He had finally left the prison where he had spent so many good years, he said.

Even Tania, who had served Ángel at Surquillo market, came with her husband. She wore a purple dress and had her hair done in a French braid. Next to her, her husband was completely invisible.

Doña Adelaida, who still sold *anticuchos* near the Plaza del Arco de Surquillo, showed up with her sister. She was catering the reception, which was to take place at Daniel's house.

Everyone seemed so happy in that moment. The dance music had already been chosen.

Ángel had wanted them to be married by Father Esteban. He had visited the prison and asked for his address. A new warden told him Esteban had been transferred to the parish of Santa Cruz in San Juan de Lurigancho. When Ángel went looking for him, he was told that Father Esteban had gone to Ayacucho. No one had heard from him since.

His friends from his wrestling days also came to the wedding. El Gordo arrived with a voucher as a wedding gift. Even El Cabo Gutarra showed up, in a suit and tie. He told Ángel that he had earned quite a bit of money in recent years and felt more settled. El Zapallo Reina, on the other hand, had vanished. Rumor had it he had run away with another wrestler and they were living together in Acapulco.

Although the reception was held at Daniel's house, Ángel told everyone that they had just made a downpayment on the apartment where they were now living.

Ángel spent the day in a state of wonder. He still could not believe that a woman—especially a woman like Julia— could even be interested, much less in love, with him and that his guests, including his brother, could experience it too. This astonishment, this joy: at his age, this should be enough to last him the rest of his life, he thought.

In the months that followed, Ángel and Julia bought a sofa, two armchairs, a lamp, a dresser, two rugs, and even a few paintings. Little by little, they furnished the living room, the bedroom, and the guest room of their apartment. Finally they had created somewhere they could live.

At the end of their first year of marriage, their son Pedro was born. Despite his age, Ángel realized for the first time that he had a paternal instinct, that inexplicable and urgent desire to gaze at his son, to protect him. He realized that, because of Pedro, he was now thinking about the future. It was a feeling he had never experienced before.

Some nights he dreamed he was swimming on the high seas after a shipwreck. It was dark, his son was floating in the black waters close by. Ángel hugged him close, held him aloft, he had to save him from drowning. The two were dragged by the dark currents. Ángel could feel himself growing weaker, but he clutched the child ever tighter.

It was a recurring dream. In the mornings when he woke, he would rush to pick up his son to make sure he was all right.

One day in the office, while checking the accounts, he scribbled something in a notebook. To have a child was to put down roots, to create a center in the world. From this center radiated the sense of routine and the future was transformed into something real. Time truly passes when there is a child nearby.

During those months, he sometimes thought of Eliana and wondered what had become of her. Once, without knowing why, he drove past the hospital where the captain had died and whispered a few words under his breath.

The situation in the country began to improve. Investments began to revitalize the economy. There were more jobs, and the middle class began to grow, especially in coastal cities. In some regions, unemployment all but disappeared, while in others, especially the rural areas in the Andes, little to nothing changed for the poor.

One of the effects of the upturn in the urban economy was an increase in passengers using public transport. Work at the company multiplied. Ángel continued to get up every morning at 5:30 a.m. to get to the office in time to hand the keys to the drivers, draw up the route map, and distribute the ticket books. He ate lunch at the kiosk, usually chicken and rice, passionfruit juice, and a flan. He feverishly drank coffee, five or six cups a day. In the evening, he would wait for the last bus to finish its shift. Then someone would come and take over. By that time, Julia would be waiting for him at home. She had given up her job to look after their son, though she sometimes gave private language lessons, which helped with the household expenses.

There was an element of risk to Ángel's job, since the

day's takings were kept in the office safe. He personally
went to deposit the money at the bank a block away.
Thankfully, he had hired Sansón, who always accompanied him. Throughout the day, the drivers and the
fare collectors would turn in their takings together with
their ticket books. Señorita Amanda, who had replaced
Julia, took charge of counting the money and giving each
driver a signed receipt. Then, most of the money would
be stored in the safe until 5 p.m. The bank closed at 6. The
main problem was counting so much money, given that
passengers invariably paid with coins.

After many years with the company, Señora Norma
had retired. She was happier living with her daughter
and her son-in-law, she explained.

Ángel often talked on the phone with Salvador
Ponciano. He would call him for no particular reason.
He never had anything special to say, simply wanted to
chat about what he had been doing recently (he felt he
had only done things once he had told Salvador about
them) and to ask Salvador what he had been up to. There
was a simple pleasure in talking to his friend about his
life. Ángel was not sure why he found it necessary. He
realized that Salvador understood the things he said, and
more, he understood what Ángel felt but left unsaid. One
way or another, they did not see each other often since
they lived so far apart. Salvador was working in one of his
cousin's stores out in Independencia.

"Things are going well, compadre," Salvador told
him. "I'm doing well. I sell my stuff here. And I have
the lovely Yesenia to keep me company, she's a little
young for me, but she's beautiful, my little enchantress.
I make her laugh. Sometimes I bring home candy from
the store. We're getting married soon. You know, I really

believe she's put a spell on me, I don't know what else to think."

Every night, before he went home, Ángel would talk to his brother and tell him about his day. By this point, Daniel was also running a much larger bus company in Cono Norte.

Who would have thought things would turn out like this? Daniel said. The Shining Path guerrilla war was in the past now. The problem with terrorists is that they have no sense of humor, Dionisio Zamora had once said to Ángel. But round here, all we do is make fun of everything. No one in this country takes anything seriously. How did those crazy guys ever think they could win? But we're all crazy, Ángel had said. Who knows who's craziest?

With Julia and little Pedro, Ángel set about creating his own weekend routine. On certain Sundays, when they did not visit his brother or his in-laws, Ángel would take Julia and Pedro to the Angamos mall. It was not particularly close to his house, but the very reason for going there was so as not to run into anyone they knew; Julia understood this, and that was where they would spend the day, in the stores and the children's play area. Sometimes they would eat in the vast food court and choose a movie to see in the afternoon.

Before long, it would be five years since he began working for Transportes Serpa. He no longer visited the prison since his friends there had long since left. But he had made new friends at work. Every trip, we're bringing on new passengers, Ángel told his brother. It just keeps growing. Things are going well. Next year, Pedro will start school. He can already write his alphabet. It's his birthday soon. It's amazing how quickly time passes and you don't even notice.

It all happened on a Sunday, the day of his son Pedro's birthday party. After a morning spent kissing and cuddling in the bedroom, Ángel and Julia emerged to tidy the living room. By noon, the table was set. The guests arrived shortly afterward. The day before, they had bought a chocolate cake, as well as some glasses and jugs (from the store where Ángel had once worked in Surquillo, where they were served by a red-headed boy). They had invited Julia's parents, Daniel and Marissa and their children, and a few friends from Pedro's kindergarten. Julia had made *ají de gallina* with rice, fried cassava with *huancaína* sauce, and a tomato, lettuce, and avocado salad. As if that were not enough, Ángel came back from the restaurant on the corner with a platter of *ceviche*. Julia's parents brought a little remote-controlled car with lights and a siren for their grandchild. Daniel, Marissa, and their children arrived with bottles of beer. Then Pedro's little friends began to arrive with gifts, clutching their parents' hands.

After lunch, everyone sat around chatting. The presents were opened, everyone sang "Happy Birthday," and, later, the parents of Pedro's friends arrived to collect their children. Only a little boy named Mariano was left, and after a while his parents came to pick him up too.

Ángel suggested his brother and his in-laws join them at the cinema. As he had expected, they politely declined, and headed home.

Ángel was left alone with his family. He and Julia tidied up the house, put out Pedro's clothes for kindergarten the next morning, and headed off to the movies, anticipating a happy ending to a wonderful and exhausting weekend. They arrived at the Angamos mall just in time for a 6:15 p.m. screening.

When they came out of the movie (a story about a boy with magical powers who flies over mountains and rescues a pale, blonde princess), Ángel suggested they get something to eat from the food court, preferably a hamburger with fries and a salad. Pedro obviously liked the idea. It seemed a fitting end to their celebrations.

Sunday evening at the mall's vast food court was always the same. People of all ages lined up at stalls and reappeared with multicolored trays while others sat waiting for them at tables. A few groups of children were running around laughing or crying, or sometimes both at once. The children, dressed in Spider-Man or Minnie Mouse T-shirts, scurried around like little animals. The edge of the food court was a succession of huge colored signs featuring the logos of Inca Kola, Kentucky Fried Chicken, and Domino's Pizza, among others. The sodas, the burgers, the Chinese food and sandwiches, the lights and the music, the usual clamorous joy of families who went out on Sundays to celebrate the sacrament of their union . . .

They were lucky because, as they entered the food court, a group of overweight parents and children were just leaving a table. Ángel and Pedro sat down and Julia asked what they wanted.

Ángel saw a group of women laughing together on the far side of the food court. They seemed happy and were moving in a slow procession, heading toward a passageway that probably led to a row of stores.

Julia jotted down Ángel's order, a hamburger and a

lemonade, and said she would return soon. Pedro got up to go with her.

"You save the table and we'll be right back," Julia said.

Ángel leaned back in his chair and looked toward the other side of the food court, where another family had just sat down.

At every table, there were three or four people.

But at one table, on the edge of the crowd, Ángel saw someone sitting alone.

At first, he could make out only a slim silhouette. Then the figure became clearer. The woman was wearing a black dress and her hands were resting on the table. She did not have a tray, a bottle, or a plate in front of her. She had only a plastic cup. She was sitting, gazing at nothing in particular, scarcely moving.

Ángel stared, his eyes fixed on her. She seemed much further away, her face seeming to hover, motionless, beyond the mass of bodies. He watched her sip from her cup.

Although much time had passed, she was easily recognizable: the long hair falling around her shoulders, the narrow waist, the eyes hard as shards of glass. It was the same figure he had last seen years before, on the night she killed the man.

Perhaps it was a coincidence, but the dark dress was the one she had been wearing the first day she came into the store. She was sitting with her legs crossed, looking sideways, focused on the cup of water balanced near the edge of the table, which looked like a small man about to commit suicide. Her posture was relaxed, she seemed to be resting after a long day's work. She did not seem out of place in these surroundings. And yet, Ángel sensed that her face had come a long way to materialize here, alone in the middle of the throng, a great distance from those around her.

By chance, Julia and Pedro were standing in line not far from her, in a pool of light. Pedro was asking his mother for something and Julia was saying no and patting his head. It was instantly apparent that Eliana knew perfectly well that Ángel's wife and son were nearby as she continued to sip from the cup and stare into the distance. One of her hands rested on the table; she moved it very slightly from time to time.

Despite his growing fear, Ángel could not take his eyes off her. He was waiting for her to turn and look at him.

In the area where she was sitting, the light was not as bright as it was inside the large circle. To one side, there were a few derelict food stands, some electrical cables and steel poles left over from some refurbishment, and behind, a large, grimy window overlooking the avenue. As always in the food court of a shopping mall still under construction, there was a dark area filled with rubble where the spotlights did not reach. Meanwhile, closer to him, the fluorescent signs from the stalls selling hamburgers, sodas, and grilled chicken shimmered with unusual intensity, as though trying to entice the diners.

Suddenly, Ángel became aware of a faint melody in the background. An orchestra was playing a romantic salsa, but within the music was a voice going in a different direction from the rest. It was the voice of a stuttering singer, utterly at odds with the music of the orchestra. The sound merged with the chorus of voices from the families: mothers shouting at their children, kids looking up and screaming, toys making whirring sounds. The spontaneous chorus created by the sum of these noises

had been steadily growing, seemingly searching for some
higher point in the cavernous space, swooping and ric-
ocheting off the ceiling, where it clashed with the trum-
pets and the salsa drums.

Families continued to pour into the food court. Some
wandered in circles searching for a free table, distracted
husbands leading the way while their wives held the hand
of some implausible child. Amid this cacophonous whirl
of screams and figures, Eliana's body remained motionless, like a sculpture that had been here long before anything else.

In the midst of this loud, bright space, Ángel felt a
sort of chasm open up, the realization that the two of
them had always been on opposite sides of the circle, in
this solitude that reminded him of his former life, when
a blood-smeared figure by the roadside had pleaded
with him to look for her children. Their shared solitude
only became concrete on that Sunday, amid the clamor
of the gathered families living the humdrum routine of
their lives, while the lives of so many others whom no
one now remembered had been brutally cut short in that
other, very different clamor composed of silences piled
one upon another.

Each was alone, but each of them knew that, even
after all this time, there was still a connection between
them. Although Eliana seemed preoccupied, turned
toward one side, Ángel knew that she had seen him and
that, by being there, she wanted to tell him something,
perhaps that she had followed him, just as he used to follow her. Perhaps she also wanted to say that she knew
she had found him in that space where verbal agree-
ments melt away. They had to plunge into that silence,
seek refuge in that strange silence that had belonged

only to them ever since that man whom Ángel called the captain had ordered him to take away her body and shoot her if necessary.

Ángel continued staring at her when, suddenly, he saw something in her face change, like a sudden realization. She raised her head, turned slightly, her eyes met his and lingered there. Her bright eyes were fixed on his, while a child's voice rose above the clamor, the parents chattered, the salsa pulsed in the heavy air, the pounding footsteps carried on, so many people gathered here to assuage their conscience and that of the world. It was then that she appeared to smile, though it was not actually a smile but a curious rictus: the slow, perfect intimation of a curve in her face that barely broadened, a confirmation of her bitterness that masked all the things they had left unsaid and would never say.

Ángel became aware of the profound truth relayed by the scene being played out here. He remembered his childhood home, playing marbles in the dust, a voice out in the yard connected with the neighbors' yard. Hadn't he known her, a long time ago? He was not sure, but he thought that she had played at his house in those far-off days, when they had both been children living in Ayacucho. Yes. He could almost picture her. They would have been three or four years old. Two little children who had met a few times in the barrio to play marbles and pitch-penny in the dust. Little Eliana tossing a marble into a hole in the ground, lost in that unearthly space that had separated them and had brought them together again. Of course. Ángel had spent his childhood in Ayacucho before his parents moved to Lima. His parents had left when he and his brother were still very young. Eliana had been there, out on the street, playing. She had remained behind. From some dark, forgotten place, her face slowly came back to him.

Suddenly everything seemed crystal clear.

The burden of guilt she had placed on him in handing him the pistol she had used to kill that man had not broken the bond between them. It had strengthened it. It was her action that had bound them together forever.

Eliana had known for some time that he had succeeded in setting up this family with Julia and Pedro. She knew that he had returned to this normal life after being in prison. She knew that Ángel had settled into a routine that encompassed hopes, perhaps even dreams, the ordinary, innocuous dreams of ordinary people: to save a little money, give their child a good education, build a home, feel fulfilled at work. Ángel's sense of purpose was no different from what anyone might aspire to, achieving the security that would lead to peaceful and relatively dignified old age. In the meantime, he wanted only to receive some compensation, some reward for his work. Ángel had put all his energy into achieving his goals. Working hard in Daniel's company. Raising his son, making his wife happy, and fulfilling his obligations, which, in truth, simply meant being at peace with himself. There was no other way to put it. Was he interested in anything else? It was almost embarrassing, surely? It was enough for him, enough for any ordinary person. Having a job, a family, moving forward as best he could in the world. Wasn't this enough? Wasn't it fair? His friends and family had fostered these principles in him. They had not been easy to achieve. He had worked hard for them. He had made it this far, to this Sunday, Pedro's birthday, an event that carved out a safe space in which time had no meaning and death could be ignored. Yes, he had come this far. He had a job and a family. Today was his son's birthday. He felt calm, perhaps even happy. He no longer hated himself; he no longer felt guilty. He had managed to return to normality, perhaps even to save himself. Not she. She was forever exiled from this temperate land where certainties thrive and protect its citizens. She had crossed the border, navigating icy paths and rivers infested with corpses, and she had remained on the far shore of life. She could not be there, with these people carrying trays of food and drinks, celebrating the end of another week in their comfortable lives. She had been exiled by what had happened to her, and could only watch the everyday events of the world from a distance bounded by the absence of her children and her husband, by the faces on that frozen heap of corpses where she had regained consciousness. She was still lying by that roadside, buried beneath the arms, the genitals, the entrails of the others. Other lives that she alone knew had also been exiled to this other dimension. The eyes that had witnessed such horrors were different from his eyes, and from those of all the men and women gathered here. From the depths of those eyes, Eliana gazed in amazement at the world, this inaccessible place governed by dull, predictable laws. Everything that had happened since that night had fashioned a space through which she blindly groped her way, with the absent emotions of a ghost. She had come to Lima to live with her cousins in San Juan de Miraflores; she had grown accustomed to the affection of her cousins and her aunts. She had wanted to devote herself to a religious order, had sung its hymns in the hope of finding refuge. She had taken care of her niece, only to find herself hounded once more by the man called Huarón who claimed to be her father. Yes. All this had happened.

All this had happened, and nothing had changed. For Eliana it was not just a matter of fleeing men like Huarón or seeking refuge in the kindness of her relatives. The only thing that could have saved her would have been to find a place where she could live with these memories without a past. To have had a life other than the one she was living. To go back, to be, to escape from this place. From the growing, gaping void that had engulfed her: the dank air of those nights in Ayacucho, the cold flagstones of the barracks floor, the crackling of wires connected to her genitals, the voice of someone telling her that her children were dead, the suffocating taste when she woke by the roadside where he had shot her. What could overcome the chain of memories she was forced to relive? Expiation, contrition, redemption: all those things he had sought were merely a string of meaningless words. Not one of them could reach Eliana. And yet, today, perhaps she was there because she knew something. Knew that he had helped her rid herself of that man, but most of all, knew that he had tried to find her so that she would not die, so she would know there was someone who could live for her.

The strange, unexpected truth that emerged from the silence in that food court filled with voices was that, in taking the blame for the death of the man who had abused her, he had not done *her* a favor, but himself. She could have taken responsibility for the man's death herself and no one would have blamed her. But Ángel took responsibility, and this had given him an opportunity to believe that, by serving his sentence, he had somehow paid his debt. Ángel knew that there are no debts, just as there is no blame, no reproach, and no regrets. There are only senseless, inexplicable acts that hold up a mirror, a mirror on which he wanted to inscribe the name of his guilt. The paved road where people go to expiate the sins they have committed is not the dirt track where those sins take place. Time simply widens the distance between them. But he had not been able to catch up with himself, back by the road where he had left her behind.

Just then, someone switched on more lights in the food court: spotlights that created a tunnel of light on one side of the ceiling. These lights simply accentuated the shadowy air in the corners through which the winds of time were blowing.

The food court was full. Some families were standing, waiting for others to give up their tables. Everyone was shouting and having a good time in a frenzied celebration that had something to do with the convulsive calm of the weekend.

In that moment, Ángel understood the story behind all the things that had happened. It seemed incredible that he had not realized before. His story was not going to end here. In fact, it would endlessly start over. Everything that had happened had been part of a plan devised by Eliana.

Their meeting when she came into his store had not come about by chance. Chance had nothing to do with it. She had tracked him down. She had known that Ángel worked there. She had traced him to Surquillo market. She had found out that he sometimes ate lunch nearby and always went back to work at the same time. She had dressed and waited for him, had come into the store to talk to him about the glasses she wanted to buy. It was she who had prompted the trip to the church hall next to her house on Calle Alipio Ponce. She had known about his time in prison, his appeal, the efforts made by his attorney, his brother's visits. She knew about his submissiveness, his reluctance to accuse her, his conversations with his friends. She knew about the three years he had spent inside, about his new job, his marriage to Julia. It occurred to Ángel that she had probably talked about him with Father Esteban. They were both from Ayacucho. This explained why Esteban had disappeared.

Only in this moment did he finally see things clearly. The story was very different from what he had believed. If Cholo Palacios had not wanted to talk, it was because he felt guilty. He, too, knew what she had planned. After she survived, after she moved to Lima, after she got in touch with her aunt and her cousins, Eliana had tracked down Cholo Palacios, had turned up at his office one morning, perhaps given him a little money. Only now did Ángel understand. That first day Ángel had gone to see him, Cholo had said that someone had been asking about him. That someone was Eliana. Cholo had been her accomplice. Thanks to Cholo, she had tracked Ángel down to the store selling glassware and crockery, she had found out his address, she had been following him that day, perhaps for several days, and on the afternoon when they met, she had steeled herself to go and see him at the market. She had stood there, waiting for her journey into the past to begin, she had stepped into the homewares store to look at him, to see him up close as he faced the truth that time was finally about to reveal, but this time it was she who was standing over him, like a judge. He had been beneath her, offering to sell her the glasses in his store. In the old station wagon he used to drive, he had been completely at her mercy, Eliana could have killed him right there in the driver's seat where their memories had once again converged. This was what she had been planning for some time, and he would have deserved it.

In that moment, everything seemed to make sense. Perhaps Eliana had not known what she would do when she saw him. Then, when he began to hound her, she must have come up with the idea to gift him with the crime. There was somber generosity in the moment when she had placed the gun in his hand, and that moment was the price to be paid so he could continue on his journey. He had accepted it. Ángel had taken the blame for Huarón's murder, he had expiated his guilt and, in doing so, he was able in time to return to the joys of a normal life, with a job, a wife, and a son. He had made a promise to his solitude, and he believed that he had emerged from that labyrinthine purgatory having earned a place in this earthly paradise. But his forgiveness was as illusory as his guilt, as his redemption, as any form of retribution or payment. There had never been such a thing, and there could never be. Only a gesture, an attempt, a hand reaching across the void.

On that Sunday afternoon, as he waited for Julia and Pedro to come back to the table, as the clamorous communion of families carried on, Eliana had appeared, just as she had in the store some years earlier with a few questions about what she was going to buy. She had once again tracked him down to remind him that they were still united, still bound by that night when he had shot her, by the silence of his refusal to help her when she had pleaded for her children and he could think only that the captain would be waiting for him. The fact that she could never return to the world was not simply his fault, nor that of the soldiers, nor that of the Shining Path guerrillas who had killed her family, nor Huarón who had abused her. It was also something that neither she nor he could understand. It was life as it had unfurled for her, being born in that godforsaken corner of the world, in a house that was little more than a shack, in the cold air of the hill overlooking hell itself.

She was a *waqcha*; she had always been an orphan. A childhood spent in a hovel in a tiny village, abandoned to poverty, where she had fashioned a shelter from cardboard boxes and blankets riddled with holes. The icy mornings when people would wake up to the hunger of knowing there would be nothing to eat all day. The dirt floor, the dry mud walls, the faces of her siblings next to her. Death peering through the window from the day she was born, leaning over the side of her crib, dooming her to that dawn when she was dumped in the long grass with her dead husband and her missing children, waking to a stream of ditch water coursing over her, stumbling toward a farmhouse, traveling to Lima, getting by as best she could in the city. The road where he had abandoned her that night had still not reached its end, it would never end. That road that had turned into the path by which she escaped, into the highway she had taken to reach the fog-bound capital, into the sidewalks she had walked with her niece and her sister on Calle Alipio Ponce. This road had extended into the spaces where she wandered in circles, searching for her children, knowing that they might still be in some dark corner. This road had no destination. She had always been a traveler of the wind, one that kept blowing toward a fate that had nothing to do with her, on a journey in which she was traveling backward, toward a place from which she could not look forward. A traveler constantly forced to look out at the road of her past, where her children still gamboled and looked at her and played together.

To endure was to ask questions, and Ángel understood the question he could see now in Eliana's eyes. Why had no one stopped the soldiers from going into her house and taking her away? Why had no one been able to stop her from being tortured that night, while the soldiers laughed at her, tortured her, and left her for dead? Why had no one stopped the terrorists from killing her children and her husband? Yes. Someone should have stopped all these things, should have been able to avert that shitty war, the horrors of those pestilential paths, the severed heads, the explosions that launched birds into the air, the blood-stained torsos hung with signs reading "This is how dogs die." Someone should have been able to prevent the swinging bodies of the men that Shining Path left hanging from trees, their testicles dangling from their mouths, the eyes of the wives and children left behind. Someone should have been able to stop the filth in the barracks, the howls in the darkness, the torture of faces submerged in buckets of urine, the sobs of women subjected to electric shocks to their breasts and iron bars shoved into their vaginas as they listened to raucous laughter. Someone should have been able to give these people the chance of a decent life in which to decide how to spend their days; a place where they could wake up without fear; enough to eat in the morning, a job where they could work with dignity, a home where they could feel warm as winter drew in. Someone should have been able to prevent these people from being born into poverty, disregarded by everyone, abandoned by the government and the authorities that lined their pockets with all the money in the world while, on their doorstep, their own people were born, destined for death, for a slow agonizing death.

Yes. Someone should have been able to prevent all these things, but Eliana did not know who. There was no office where she could go to lodge a complaint about her life. Should she complain to the army, the terrorists, the governor of Lima, to the mayor, the ministers, the officials, the president? Perhaps. But what would it achieve? Was there anyone to whom she could complain? She had been born in a part of the world where people are less than nothing, a place where it is difficult even to contemplate those who stroll through streets and offices, who get in and out of the cars that hurtle along elevated motorways. Ángel had tried to do something to help her, but also to help himself. He had tried, perhaps knowing that it would not work. And if that hard, bitter expression she was giving him, that glare of icy madness, lingered a second longer, he would have to go over to her and say something, to tell her that he would never measure up to her ordeal, but that he wanted her to understand. To know that, since that night when he had abandoned her, when he had refused to look for her children, when he had shot her and left her for dead amid a pile of corpses by the roadside, she had become the most important person in his life. Something she always would be. That tonight, here in the shopping mall, as families bustled about with their trays, he realized she had emerged from that darkness to remind him of that fact. A voice came from that dark figure and hovered in the air: it is thanks to me you are here, with your family, it said. And, only in that moment did Ángel realize that something had happened between them back when they were children, back when he and his parents were living on the Jirón Las

Azucenas de Ayacucho, before he had come to school in Lima. New images began to flood back. Marbles in the dust, a little girl with braids, a faint voice coming from a window. The flux of time brought these pictures back to him. The face of that man he called the captain found its way into the series of images.

The past was a vertical shaft, with sharp walls. The voice had lingered in that house only to reappear in the silence of anonymous voices in the open air. He had tried to defy the past. In the ring, facing down other fighters, he had tried to fight the man he had once been. He had tried to use his fists to destroy other bodies, never knowing that it was his own body confronting him. He had talked to the captain, who could no longer hear him or understand him. He had sat in his store and, without knowing, he had waited for Eliana. He had dreamt that he woke every morning to a room filled with cracks and an ache in his back. He had recounted everything and even asked advice of the dead mother he might have saved had he paid attention on a long-ago afternoon. For a split-second he felt the urge to bring together Daniel and Marissa, his niece and nephew, to speak to his mother again, tell his story to El Gordo, Salvador Ponciano, Father Esteban, Sinesio, and Dimas Donayre. To tell them everything. Bring them all together so he could tell them, could ask them. Memories have many masks that reveal our true faces: a mass of flesh and bone without form or features. It is possible to struggle against memories, but not the past.

But in that same moment, some way along the journey through the years and the silences amplified by Eliana's gaze, out of the depths of the clamor that protected them, Ángel sensed an unexpected softening in her expression on the far side of the circle, a sadness of lines revealed for the first time. Perhaps what she was trying to project was her appreciation (that was one way of putting it), her acknowledgment of his efforts on her behalf. It was not a pardon, gratitude, or reconciliation; there was nothing of that. Perhaps she did not feel happy at seeing him with his wife and child in his stable life. Or perhaps it neither bothered her nor made her happy. She was a long way from thanking him for taking the blame for murdering the man who had stalked her. She was not grateful for his guilt or his regret or his intentions. Gratitude had nothing to do with what was happening.

Ángel was still gazing at her, in her plastic chair, with her beaker of water in front of her, when her face began to move. She was talking under her breath, saying something to him in that moment, her eyes fixed on him.

Ángel did not hear her words but he could see her lips move, he could clearly make that out. Yes. She had said the words. He had wanted to do something after all, and somewhere in her face she was acknowledging that. She was saying that this was the last time they would see each another, that she was leaving him with this final gesture, which was not one of pain, or hatred, or sadness, but the kind of dispassionate serenity that could exist only on the other shore of life, which she would never leave. This would be their last encounter, a happy ending of a sort after so many moments in the dark of the earth and guttural voices. And it would have to be enough, even if he would not accept it.

Because at a certain point, after Julia and Pedro reappeared with a tray laden with sandwiches, fries, and lemonade, after Julia asked whether he wanted a sachet of mayonnaise, and said that, knowing him as she did, she had bought him a black coffee, after his son had climbed onto his lap, after Julia placed a napkin next to him, Ángel had set Pedro down and begun to walk toward Eliana. He walked slowly. Walked through the throng of anonymous bodies with their trays and their children. At some point, he felt as though he had left behind the clamor and entered a universe where there was no sound, close to the table where she was sitting, gazing at nothing in particular.

Suddenly, a group of families with trays stepped in front of him. Someone was saying, "If you get in this line, I'll get in the one over there." A group of children cleaved the air in front of him, and Ángel was forced to stop. The shimmering signs on the food stands beat down on his face with unexpected brilliance.

Then he looked again at the table where Eliana had been sitting.

He could see no one.

The table was empty. Nor had there been anyone sitting there, which was curious since so many people were waiting for tables. He had not seen her go out through any of the doors. Eliana had vanished.

There was no one but him, standing amid the commotion of families making their way through this Sunday, bound for somewhere. For many, it was already getting late. The escalators were thronged with families. Some had begun to leave, thinking about a house with a living room and a television where they could prolong their dreams and their omissions.

Ángel stood, motionless. Suddenly he felt his son's hand in his. Still he stared at the far shore of the space.

"What's wrong, Papá? Why did you leave?"

Ángel turned to him. Then looked back at the empty table.

"Nothing. I thought I saw somebody."

The little boy looked toward the far end of the space.

"Who? Who did you see?"

Ángel turned on his heel. Together, they walked back to the table where Julia was waiting. They sat down. She took his hand.

"Is everything all right?"

Ángel hoisted Pedro onto his lap. He looked at her.

"Yes. We're going to be fine."

Acknowledgments

Books such as *Memoria y batallas en nombre de los inocentes*, by Ernesto de la Jara; *Entre prójimos*, by Kimberley Theidon, and *When Rains Became Floods: A Child Soldier's Story*, by Lurgio Gavilán Sánchez (translated by Margaret Randall), provided invaluable information and accounts of unique experiences and reflections that have inspired many of the episodes in this novel. I owe these authors a profound debt of gratitude.

The same is true of *Muerte en el Pentagonito*, by Ricardo Uceda; *Sendero. La guerra milenaria en el Perú*, by Gustavo Gorriti, and *El surgimiento de Sendero Luminoso*, by Carlos Iván Degregori. I would also like to offer my special thanks to Ernesto de la Jara, José Luis Pérez Guadalupe, and Antonio Astoray Terrones for their invaluable personal help. Readers, including Federico de Cárdenas, Germán Coronado, and Francisco Lombardi offered valuable comments on the novel. Finally, a number of interviews conducted in Lima and in Ayacucho, with former soldiers of the Ejército y la Marina del Perú who were stationed in the area, were also a great source of inspiration and encouragement. During the Shining Path war, a number of Peruvian soldiers and officers committed abuses, but many behaved heroically in the face of the terrorists, for which Peruvians must always be grateful.

To my wife Kristin, for her patience, her encouragement, and her comments, my deepest love.

About the Author and Translators

ALONSO CUETO
Lima, Peru
Cueto is the author of over twenty books, including novels, short-story collections, and essays. Cueto was awarded the 2000 Anna Seghers Prize, the 2005 Premio Herralde, and the 2019 Premio de Narrativa Juan Goytisolo, among several other distinctions. His novels have been translated into sixteen languages.

FRANK WYNNE
Sligo, Ireland
Wynne is a writer and literary translator whose authors include Michel Houellebecq, Virginie Despentes, and Javier Cercas. His translations have earned him the IMPAC Prize, the Independent Foreign Fiction Prize, and the Scott Moncrieff Prize. His translation of Alonso Cueto's novel *The Blue Hour* won him the Premio Valle Inclán in 2013.

JESSIE MENDEZ SAYER
Mexico City, Mexico
Mendez Sayer is a literary translator, editor, and former literary scout. She studied history and Spanish at the University of Edinburgh.